CELIA FINDS AN ANGEL

A Romp Through St Urith With Well

GLENDA BARNETT

Copyright @ 2018 Glenda Barnett

No part of this book may be reproduced in any form or by any electronic or mechanical means, including information storage and retrieval systems without written permission from the author, except for the use of brief quotations in a book review.

This is a work of fiction. Names, characters, businesses, places, events and incidents are either the product of the author's imagination or used in a fictitious manner. Any resemblance to actual persons, living or dead, or actual events is purely coincidental.

Sign up to the Celia Ladygarden blog to hear about new releases and everyday life in the Ladygarden household at
www.celialadygarden.com

'I saw the angel in the marble and carved until I set him free.'
Michelangelo.

Prologue

The young girl, delirious with the crippling pain, groaned on the narrow truckle bed she shared, top to tail, with the other maid. Some of her hair had escaped from its night-time plait and was hanging around her face like a rat's tail as sweat dripped off her brow.

'Mother?' Oh, how she wanted her here. Her dear mother's gentle loving face swum in front of her eyes in the pitch darkness. 'Oh, mother,' the girl groaned and grasped her stomach through her thin cotton night-dress. Terrified at the realisation of what was happening to her, she cried out.

'Ada? What's wrong?' asked Edna sitting up as wisps of her coarse dark hair stuck up around her small, pale, frightened face. 'Hush,' she said, reaching across from her end of the bed and trying to hold down Ada's flapping arms.

'Pain, grrrr... feel sick,' groaned the girl in reply.

'Please, Ada, stop making that noise! You'll have Cook down here in a minute. What shall I do? I'll fetch 'ee a glass of water.' Edna stepped out onto the cold cobbled floor of the basement, hastily slipped her shoes on and wrapped her knitted shawl about her shoulders.

It wasn't truly cold but it wasn't warm either. The mistress had instructed the gardeners to put up some wooden partitions around a corner of the basement, forming a small bedroom area and enclosing the truckle bed and the upturned box that the candle rested on. The two young maids enjoyed having their own space. Cook would never venture down here so they felt safe. Warboys would come down to fetch wine, or whatever the master ordered, but he was elderly and quite fatherly and kind to the young maids.

After lighting the stub of candle set on the metal lid from a jar, Edna picked up the wooden slop bucket from the corner of the room and placed it next to the bed near Ada's head. 'Ada, if you do be sick, be sick in that bucket, but not in the bed for 'eaven's sake.'

Edna was shaking with the cold and the fear but bravely crept up the stone steps and took the latch of the oak door in her hand. Very, very, gently, as quietly as she was able, she lifted the latch cringing at the sound of the metallic click as the bar lifted and the door swung open. Please, don't wake up, please don't wake up, she repeated like a charm in her head, in dread of Cook waking up.

Cook, who ruled the kitchen with the whack of a large wooden spoon, had her own private space in a small room off the kitchen. Although it had a perfectly working door it was hidden from view by a heavy brown velvet curtain that was pulled across, concealing whether the door was open or closed. This curtain door combination was a form of torture to the maids. When Cook had gone for a lie down they had to go about their duties in an unnatural silence as they would never know if the door was open or closed. Cook would derive pleasure from pretending she had closed the door but in fact had only rattled the latch and banged it then opened it quietly.

The poor maids had been caught unawares one day when they had thought cook had closed the door and was having a nap. They had finished washing the pots and pans, which took twice as long when you weren't allowed to make a noise, and they were scrubbing the floor. It was back-breaking work and to make it easier they had devised a game where they would start at opposite sides of the kitchen and see who could get to the center first. This time they had started scrubbing diagonally across the kitchen and when Ada had reached the large pine table she found half a lemon behind one of the huge pine legs. Without thinking, she picked it up and threw it at Edna's head. Surprised, Edna sat back on her heels, hand to head. When she saw Ada laughing at her she looked around to see what had hit her and, finding the lemon, had thrown it back.

Although they tried to contain their giggles, it just got worse. They both fell over onto the floor, tears rolling down their cheeks.

The curtain was flung back and the harsh sound of the curtain rings scraping along the pole instantly stopped the girl's laughter. They got back on their knees and grabbed their scrubbing brushes and vigorously scrubbed the flagstone floors.

'You wicked girls! How dare you wake me up! You know how hard I work, I need my rest!' all this was said with a whack of the wooden spoon on every word.

Edna stood in the dark doorway, listening. Once she knew all was well she started creeping across the flagstone kitchen floor, casting a glance across to the curtained door. She couldn't see or hear any movement, so continued to the china sink. Next to the sink were the kettles and pans filled with water ready for the next morning's breakfast. Her heart was thumping in her chest. Never had she dared leave the basement and enter the kitchen after bedtime. As carefully and quietly as she could she filled a wooden cup with water from one of the saucepans, then retraced her steps back to the basement.

Ada was groaning and thrashing about. Edna hurried down the steps with the water, terrified that Cook would hear and wake up. She would have to keep Ada quiet somehow. With a good degree of effort, she managed to haul Ada up into a sitting position and get her to sip some water, but she was frightened and didn't know what else to do until Ada spoke.

'Fetch Barnabas, Edna, tell him I'm ill and I need him. If he refuses tell him that you will have to wake Sir Rufus if he doesn't come with you.' Ada threw herself back on the bed with a low moan.

'The young master! Ada, what are you saying? I cannot go to his room, you must be mad! I'll be sent home in disgrace.'

'Edna, I'm dying, 'ee be the only one that can help me, please go and fetch him?' Ada begged as her eyes filled with tears that spilled out and rolled down her flushed cheeks.

Edna was shaking and now felt sick herself. She was only thirteen, two years younger than Ada. Ada was her friend and had become like a sister to her as she was only allowed to visit her family every three months, even though they lived in the nearby village.

It was Ada who had taken her under her wing when she arrived at Stonepark, helped her with her duties and protected her from Cook as much as she was able. She had no idea what was wrong with Ada but she would do anything to save her, but could she bring herself to knock on the young master's door? She stood for a moment, unsure, then another groan from Ada sent her, once again, out of the basement.

Ada, overwhelmed with relief that Barnabas had come, was glad of his arms supporting her across the yard, but she was confused as to why were they heading for the stables? Once they were in an empty stable Barnabas let go of her without warning. In her weakened state she stumbled and put her hand on the rough wall to support herself, not sure how long she could remain on her feet. Barnabas had fetched a horse blanket which he threw down onto the straw next to her. As another pain gripped her, she lowered herself down onto the rough woollen blanket on the stable floor and looked up at Barnabas but before she could speak he said,

'How could you have been so stupid, sending that milksop to my room. If my mother and father had woken up you'd be lying in the workhouse now and I would have been packed off to my aunt Griffiths on Bodmin Moor!'

'I didn't know what was wrong with me at first but now I know, Barnabas. You've got to help me, I don't know why you've brought me out here... Barnabas, it hurts, you've got to help me.'

'You stupid bitch, I can't help you!' Barnabas shouted back as he strode up and down the stable. 'How could you have let this happen?'

'I'm sorry, Barnabas, but this is your child. Surely Sir Rufus wouldn't want his grandson to be born in a stable?' Ada protested before another strong pain gripped her.

'You strumpet! I doubt the bastard child is mine. I bet you spread your legs for every man within a mile.' Barnabas left the stable banging the door closed behind him and plunging the sobbing girl into the blackest of black, with the only sound the soft snicker from the horse in the next stable.

Lying on the wet blanket, Ada had torn off a piece

off her nightgown to wrap the small mewling bundle in. Its cries were growing weaker but she didn't have the strength to pick it up. Hope flared in her heart as she heard Barnabas's footsteps approach the stable. He was coming back! The door opened and light flooded in from the nearly full moon. Barnabas was returning for her. She tried to tidy her hair which hung lank and wet about her face. Summoning up all her energy she tried to lift herself up off the floor but only managed to sit up enough to lean her weight back on her two elbows.

The love in Ada's eyes turned to shock as Barnabas thrust the three prongs of the pitchfork into her chest, puncturing her heart and lungs.

He dragged the horse blanket with its grisly content across the yard and into the kitchen, pausing in the middle of the room to listen for any sounds from Cook's room. Cook's gin aided snores reassured him and he continued towards the large ornate fireplace. It took him awhile to find the switch. He hadn't used it since he was a child, but eventually there was a click and the whole of the fireplace swung out into the room revealing a small barrel-roofed space. Sweat broke out under his armpits as he fought to place the blanket and its contents as deep into the space as it would go. As he started to push the fireplace back into place he heard a faint mewling coming from the horse blanket, but it was not strong enough to be heard once the gap had been closed tight. Now there was the other girl to deal with.

Barnabas stripped off and climbed into bed. What a

lucky escape. What a ruckus there would be when it was discovered that the two kitchen maids had run off together, and what's more they had stolen a set of silver spoons. He laughed at the anticipation of his mother's histrionics on finding out in the morning.

Angels Calling

❧❧❧

'Help, help!' still echoed in Celia's consciousness as she fumbled for the bedside light and tapped it, bringing it to life. She lay there for a moment, heart pounding with the remnants of the nightmare that had awoken her. It was bit like that weird Doctor Who story with all those scary Weeping Angels, she thought. Celia's dream angel wasn't as scary as those, but the angel was asking for help. She had been having the same angel dream for the past few months and it was beginning to get on her nerves, but she had always had an open mind regarding the supernatural believing, as Shakespeare said, 'Many a thing twixt heaven and earth.'

From when she was very young she had experienced 'moments' as her mother had called them. It was more than the sixth sense or gut instinct that most people have, such as knowing who was calling on the phone or being wary of certain people. She sometimes

9

really knew things she could not possibly know. For Celia it was like picking up a faint thread of a story, almost like a radio wave, a mist drifting through her mind, but occasionally she experienced such a strong feeling that she would feel quite agitated. Sometimes she would have such a feeling of dread that she would find it difficult to enter a house, as if the very fabric of the building had soaked up sorrow or fear. Celia had become used to these feelings over the years and would let them go unless it was a feeling about a member of her family, then she would text or ring to make sure they were alright. Her family often referred to her as a witch but in a good way she hoped.

This thing with the angels was different. Not only was she dreaming of them, she kept seeing angels. Not real angels of course, she wasn't going loopy. No, it was things like angel candles, or statues and naff angel garden ornaments. In fact, she had bought a faux plaster bird nesting box with an angel sitting on the top, wings spread, from one of the bargain stores in Barnstaple, that were seemingly springing up in every town. It hadn't lasted long after Ronald and her grandson had decided to use it as a target for their catapults in the garden. She saw angels on the covers of books, pictures of angels, it seemed as if they were everywhere. Even the water company surveyor visiting for putting in a water meter (if Celia could train Ronald into not rinsing everything within an inch of its life they might save some money!) called her Angel. Of course, it was very likely that the more she thought about them, the more she would notice them but Celia was beginning to think it was a sign of something or other. Celia believed in signs.

'You still reading?' asked a grumpy voice the other side of Hirsute Roley. 'I can't sleep with that light on.' Within seconds Ronald had turned over and was snoring as loud as a John Deere tractor. Typical! Thought Celia, turning the light off and covering her ears to block out the noise. Ronald was no angel. A dig in the ribs quietened him down, but not for long. The last thoughts she had before visiting the land of nod was of Ruby Bins.

Bin Gin

C elia had popped into see Ruby earlier that day to give her some wool that she'd had over from knitting her granddaughter a cardigan. Ruby welcomed any donations as she liked to knit blankets for charity. She would knit up squares in a rainbow of colours, join them together and send them to the Knit for Peace charity. * Ruby Bins lived above her daughter Betty's bakery, 'Betty Bins Buns & Batch'. Betty only made two products, rock buns and batch loaves, using recipes passed down in the Bins family. 'If it was good enough for my dad and his dad before him, it's good enough for me,' Betty would say if anyone dared to suggest she might like to expand her repertoire. Unbeknownst to all but a few close friends, Betty did in fact make one more product, Bin Gin. According to Ruby's husband's forebears it was produced for medicinal purposes for arthritis. Ruby's rule was that you eat the raisins to prevent arthritis and you eat the raisins to relieve the symptoms of arthritis, either way was a benefit. Ruby, after some consideration and discussion with Betty and Dusty, has kindly agreed that Celia can share the secret recipe with you. It's in the back of the book but she asks that you please keep it a secret.

That morning Celia had climbed the stairs up to Betty's home above the Bakery and knocked before opening the door into Ruby's room. Her eyes, as usual, were drawn across the room to the large bay window with its view looking over the village. She smiled at Ruby sitting in her comfy upholstered chair with its traditional antimacassars. From her vantage point, Ruby would keep a firm eye on the goings on in the village and would always have a juicy tidbit of gossip to share, not that Celia liked to gossip. Ruby was screwing the top back on her jar of Bin Gin and licking her lips after taking her morning nine raisins from the jar.

'Ello my lovely, will 'ee pick up thikky ole skriddicks and duzz' bunnies fer 'ee maid? Tiz makin' the plaace look praper bissly. If us's geets down there us'll never geet up. I need our Betty to dust 'n'all me squinches.' Ruby pointed to the offending fluffballs lying on the sun-soaked floor.

'My floors are like yours Ruby, no carpets. When the sun shines across the surface, it shows up the dust something chronic and every time there's a breath of wind it bowls the dust bunnies along like tumbleweed,' Celia said as she bent down and picked up some of the offending dust and fluff ball.

'There 'ee goes, 'ee be up to summut, I know's it,' Ruby said looking out of her window.

'Who do you mean Ruby?' Celia asked, craning her neck out of the window and just managing to catch a glimpse of the back view of a smartly dressed man turning into The Unfurled Moth.

'That there incomer fella, I bleeve 'ee cum fum Lunnan.' replied Ruby with a look that instantly denigrated the poor chap and probably shrunk his man-bits.

'Oh, I know who you mean Ruby, his name is Max Cheetham. I'll admit nobody seems to know what he is doing here (which is odd, as everybody knew everything about everybody in St Urith, Celia thought) but you can't assume ee's up to summut, I mean up to something.'

'I see's what I see's and I know's what I know's, ee's up to summut, you'm mark my words.' Ruby folded up her mouth till her lips almost reached her nose and the ends nearly reached her chin. It wasn't so much a pursed mouth as a gin-trap.

What was Max Cheetham doing in the village? Celia asked herself, as she went back down the stairs to the bakery below. I think I'd better have a chat with him and see what I can find out. Nobody else in the village has managed to find out yet, maybe Ruby was right about him. She may spend most of her time in her flat above the bakery but she had her eye on the village, the wisdom of age and was a fair judge of people. Ruby hadn't mentioned Max's sometime drinking companion

Monty Butler, another newcomer to the village, I wonder what she thinks of him...

THE BONES LAY UNDISTURBED in the darkness, the Angel of Presence watching over them.

MAX CHEETHAM SLID the key into the lock, turned it and opened his front door as quietly as he could. Max was an increasingly nervous man, who was beginning to believe that he was out of his depth.

Before he entered the cottage, he looked up and down the lane, closing the door just as the dawn broke over the hill.

Invasion of the Celts

Hunkering down to access the bottom shelves the two women whispered conspiratorially but loud enough for Celia to recognise their strong Welsh accents. Celia was in the charity shop looking for some everyday tea plates. She had found some she'd liked in a previous charity shop at fifteen pounds for six but had walked away thinking how ridiculous, that was almost the price of brand new ones! Just because they labelled everything vintage they thought they could charge a fortune. Daft, thought Celia crossly, they get everything given for free and surely, they would sell more if their prices were reasonable. Then she came over all guilty for being mean. She was now in a less vintage and more charity shop and had found two sets of plates that were 'possibles'. Then she spotted a rather funky set from the 70's which she suspected were of German design and picked one up for perusal. It was at this point that she felt the invasion of the Welsh.

Down at knee level the two women crouched and crept, crab-like, towards her. The nudge at Celia's knee was only the initial foray into combat. It was followed up by firm pressure - these ladies were pro's. Before she knew it, she was at least three feet away from the plates and the two Welsh crabs in their fleece bodywarmers, jeans and 'Per Una' tee-shirts were rummaging glee-fully in a box of cutlery on the bottom shelf. Standing there resting her knees against a pale blue fleece with a second-hand tea-plate in her hand, Celia got the giggles and thought what am I doing? I have perfectly good tea-plates at home, classic Denby, why on earth am I saving them for best? At my age when is there going to be a 'best' time? Reaching across the Welsh woman, trying to replace the tea-plate, she had almost reached the shelf when the pale blue fleece rose up and Celia found herself piggy-backing a Celt.

Celia's first instinct was to cling on, not wanting to drop the tea plate and break up the set. The surprised Celt thought she was being attacked and swung around thereby crashing Celia into her companion. The poor woman was completely unaware of what was going on behind her and was happily sorting through the cutlery when she received a violent shunt from behind, pitching her head-first into the cutlery box. This resulted in her doing a half handstand, her bum flew up in the air then hit the underside of the shelf above breaking the supports, leaving her legs sticking out at right-angles. The shelf which had three sets of tea-plates on was now balancing precariously on her arse.

Time seemed suspended. There was silence as everyone in the shop turned to see what all the commotion was. What they saw was a frozen tableau.

Celia, still clinging onto the back of a woman in the blue fleece, her legs wrapped around and clutching on for dear life and a second woman with her head in a box of cutlery, and her arse supporting a wobbling shelf of rattling tea-plates. Chaos and noise erupted as the woman in the blue fleece started screaming and her friend in the box started yelling, 'Helpu! Helpu! Helpu!' The manager of the charity shop joined in the shouting causing her assistant an elderly lady of a nervous disposition to put her hands over her ears saying, 'Oh my, oh my oh my,' over and over again as she went around in tight little circles.

Celia knew she had to act. She slid off the back of the Welsh woman in the pale blue fleece and pulled on her arm, turning her around before slapping her soundly on the face. She knew that's what you had to do when someone has hysterics. Unfortunately, it seemed to have the opposite effect and the woman started screaming even louder. By this time the manager had run around from the other side of the counter to help. The woman in the cutlery box was moaning 'I'm going...I'm...' as her legs began to droop.

The manager nodded at Celia, 'You grab the other end of the shelf,' and 'You,' to a man in a bright green anorak and carrying a red Devon Air Ambulance shopping bag with a pink bra hanging out of it, 'You grab her legs.'

Celia grabbed the end of the shelf, the manager the other and together they carefully laid it on the floor. Then they went to assist the poor woman with her head in the box. Anyone looking in the window would probably assume she was doing some form of extreme Yoga, possibly the downward dog, thought Celia, suddenly struck by the humour of the situation and trying to suppress the giggles she could feel bubbling up. The Welsh woman with her head in the cutlery box was quite sturdy and it took some effort from Celia, the Manager and the green anoraked man (who, ironically, was also clutching a second-hand Superman tee-shirt and a blue striped teapot) to lower her legs down to the ground and get her upright. The green anoraked man tossed the t-shirt nonchalantly over his shoulder freeing up one arm to grab a portion of the stricken Welsh woman. There was one dodgy moment when the lid of the teapot threatened to come adrift but after a careful bit of balancing it was managed. Apart from a little shock the woman was completely unharmed. Luckily, she was wearing a homemade beret made out of what appeared to be a pink welsh blanket. It was the perfect air-cushion. After a quick explanation and a donation of five pounds to the charity, Celia made a hasty escape from the charity shop sans tea plates. Grabbing the door handle, the sleeve of her cardigan became hooked on the wing of a silver coloured angel ornament hanging on the door. 'Frigging hell!'

Dog's Breakfast

It had been a funny sort of day she thought as she drove home looking forward to taking hirsute Roley and Polly out for walk. A bit of fresh air is just what she needed to clear her head of this morning's embarrassment. The day hadn't started well. This morning instead of her normal porridge, dried fruits and honey (good for her brain she believed) Celia had decided unusually to have some toast. It was the smell of Ronald's that had made her fancy it. Ronald had finished his breakfast so she thought she'd save washing up by using his plate. She'd pulled one piece of toast from the toaster, switched it off at the plug and fished in the broken side with a fork for the second piece of toast before spreading both with real butter (Ronald couldn't abide margarine) and marmalade. She'd been halfway through eating the last half when Ronald had entered the kitchen.

'Where's the knife and the butter dish gone?' He asked.

'What knife? Celia asked.

'The one that was on the empty butter dish.' Ronald replied.

'I'm using it,' Celia said, pointing to the butter dish that she had refilled, the said knife resting upon it.

'That's the knife I used to cut up Roley's and Polly's dog food,' Ronald said.

Later, walking her fur babies, Hirsute Roley and Polly, Celia couldn't help but stop and look across at Apple Cottage as she was passing. It was about eight months ago that Colonel Cottle had been murdered and Celia had been right in the thick of it. Although she had always liked puzzles and jigsaws and was an avid reader of murder mystery books, she hadn't known she had a knack for solving murders until the death of Colonel Cottle. Although the cottage was still empty a sold notice had been tacked on to the 'For Sale' sign.

The Colonel's widow Dottie and her new husband Nico had invited Celia and Ronald out to Rhodes for a holiday. They planned to go out sometime in June next year and were excited about visiting the village where Nico's family Taverna was, that he and Dottie were now running. Celia missed Dottie, although they hadn't known each other very well before, having been thrust together in difficult circumstances they had formed a bond. Celia and Ronald had enjoyed a few happy holidays on Rhodes in the past (although there had been the snake incident) and looked forward to returning to the island.

Saggy Bottom, the cottage next door to Apple cottage had also been sold. Poor Pinky thought Celia, he'd been murdered because he'd seen too much, he hadn't deserved to die. Needless to say, there was a heap of speculation in the village about who the new people moving in might be. She walked on, Hirsute Roley stopping here and there as he found a particularly interesting scent, his walks were more sniffathons than walks. This had changed a little with the arrival of Polly, a grey and white Shih Tzu. A pure white feather floated down and landed on the back of Hirsute Roley.

'Well my lovely, what is it they say? "feathers appear when angels are near"? I think I'll keep this and stick it in one of my notebooks,' Celia said to Roley who cocked his little head on one side and raised a hairy little paw as he looked at her and considered what she had said. Polly positively bounced along with the absolute joy of being outdoors and free and Hirsute Roley, determined to be top dog, endeavoured to keep up with her. Celia and Ronald had adopted Polly who had been rescued from a puppy farm by an amazing charity called 'Many Tears Rescue'*

As she reached the junction to the main road through the village, a van rattled past, a hand vigorously waving out of the window. Celia presumed the van had an M.O.T but it must have been a close-run thing. She laughed out loud as the van passed and she watched it disappear down the road. She had heard on the village under-web that Cat (Catherine to her mother) the mobile hairdresser was doing so well that she had bought herself a second-hand van. Looking at it as it rattled down the street, Celia could clearly see Cat had repainted it herself.

Cat's Cut's

✿

C at was thrilled with her new van bought off a local online site. Now to make it her own and get some advertising at the same time. She certainly wouldn't be putting her real name on the side though. Whoever called their daughter Edna these days? Oh, she knew all about her ancestor who had gone missing from one of the big houses just outside of the village and the family tradition of the girl babies carrying on her name so that she would never be forgotten. She wouldn't have minded having Edna as a second name as her mum had wanted. Unfortunately, her dad popped into the Unfurled Moth to wet the baby's head on the way to register the birth and had swapped Catherine and Edna whilst in his cups.

The first thing she had done was to paint and customise it to advertise her business. She'd bought some paint from a cheap value shop in Bideford. A bright sunshine yellow was her chosen colour. She thought that it would be noticed as she drove around the villages. When she'd finished she stepped back paintbrush dripping, the result wasn't quite as good as she hoped but using cheap paint she hadn't expected showroom quality and she didn't have enough paint for another coat. When the paint was dry she carefully painted 'Cat's Cuts' on the side with the 'Cuts' stylishly staggered under the 'a' of 'Cat's' in a Mediterranean blue her dad had over from painting some metal garden chairs. She stepped back and admired her handiwork. She'd thought the blue a lovely contrast to the yellow. On the back doors she spent ages measuring and marking before carefully painting a giant pair of scissors in the same vivid blue. Once she had placed all her hairdressing equipment carefully inside, she was ready for business. Cat loved driving her new van and was pleased that the bright sunny yellow made people smile as she drove passed and was thrilled with all the extra business she was picking up.

Landing Lights

❧

W hat Celia saw as the brightly coloured van passed was the unfortunate name Cat's'pee Cuts.' The cheap paint Cat had used to cover the original business name of 'Speedy Motors' really hadn't been thick enough and some of the original letters were bleeding through. The back doors disappearing down the road sported not a pair of scissors as Cat had designed but what to Celia looked like a bright blue penis and a pair of matching testicles.

Carrying on with her walk Celia passed the parish hall, 'What the... Little buggers!' she said, stopping as she noticed a broken window. She pushed through the ornamental gate, made and donated by a talented and generous parishioner, and inspected the damage. Four windows broken. Luckily, they were double glazed and it was only the outside pane that was damaged leaving the inside pane intact. When she looked closer she could see a pellet which she thought might have come from a 'BB Gun' inside the broken pane.

She later learned that kids had also tried to shoot at the windows around the back of The Unfurled Moth. Willie's place backed onto the pub and his chickens had kicked up a hell of a fuss. Willie had thought there was a fox and fetched his shotgun. Unfortunately, he was wearing his pyjama bottoms, for the sight of a trouser-less Willie might have seriously damaged the little darlings for life. Fortunately, the knot had come undone on his pyjama bottoms, causing them to slip down. Willie tripped over the flapping pyjama legs and the shotgun went off. Luckily for the offending kiddiewinks Willie made his own cartridges and the shot was made of dried chicken shit!

Closing the gate behind her Celia walked on. The damaged windows would come up at the next parish hall committee meeting but there was probably no point in replacing them as there was an ongoing fundraising drive to demolish the old kitchen and committee room and build a new extension, to include disabled toilets. As the committee's new chairperson, she had been enthusiastic at first but this initial enthusiasm had faded over time with the struggle of fundraising and the steady stream of money gurgling out to pay the multitude of reports and surveys needed by the local authority. The environmental survey had discovered two occasional visiting bats, restricting the times the existing building could be demolished and the new extension built. They also had to provide a bat box for the occasional dogging bats who ventured away from the church tower. Celia, although agreeing to the principle of protecting the bats, thought it ironic that there were so many more enforcers of the rules regarding the flying mice but nobody to stop eleven and twelve-year old's using BB guns at will. Still, after the 'Willie Incident' there had been no sign of BB guns, so Willie had proved to be a bigger deterrent than the police might have been.

Leaning on the stone wall gazing out over the village playing field and the fields and farms beyond, Celia thought how lucky she was to live in such a beautiful place, with a view at every turn. She also wondered when they would be getting the landing lights for the Devon Air Ambulance, as the playing field was the designated landing site. One of the local residents Miss Worsnip, whose property was near the playing field, had raised several objections to this designated landing site. The most worrying to Miss Worsnip was the possibility of the helicopter landing on top of her. 'Them ellycops be lannen on me ouse' an' I wone' ave' it!'

The Parish Council had listened to all the legitimate concerns but as this was the only safe landing site this was where it would be. Until the village could provide the requisite landing lights the villagers had a well-practiced system in place should the need arise. This consisted of a mixture of mobile phones, hurricane lamps and, in Willie's case, a very bizarre creation made from a three-branch candelabra with three Edenproject like shades made of egg-shells, which covered and protected the flames. Very artistic was Willie. Up till now when the Devon Air Ambulance had been called to an emergency in the parish, word would spread and people would gather on the playing field. After a bit of argy-bargy and shuffling around, villagers would arrange themselves in a large circle holding aloft their mobile phones, lamps, torches and Willie his candles, guiding the helicopter down. The Devon Air Ambulance wanted as many of the small rural villages as possible to install landing lights but they came at quite a cost. Celia knew that theirs, like most of the other villages, would work their socks off to make sure the lights were put in place.

As Celia turned away from the playing field towards home she saw a movement out of the corner of her eye. Looking across to the church, she couldn't see anything at first, then she saw the back of that Max chappie. He was talking animatedly to someone but whoever it was was concealed by the wall. He must have sensed her watching because he stopped and started looking around. Celia put her head down and walked on home, wondering who he could have been talking to because as far as the gossips were concerned he had no connection with the village at all. This made her even more eager to ask him some questions.

Harold in Puce

❦

The library van rocked slightly as Harold stretched out his arm and shifted his weight to place the book on the shelf. These was where the books destined for return to the branch library sat. Just as he was about to lay the book down he noticed the corner of a piece of paper sticking out. Laying the book back down on his counter he was about to open it and investigate when Miss Worsnip stepped into the van. Harold's friendly, open, face fell and his stomach did a Monterey turn. Pushing his floppy fringe of light brown hair back off his face, he straightened up as if preparing for battle.

'You'm too busy ter' tek' me books in are you'm Harold? You'm *not* sposed ter be reading on Library time! I've a good mind ter' report you!' She slapped her two books down on the counter, narrowly missing Harold's fingers.

She was not one of Harold's favourite customers.

Apart from complaining about the selection of books available she always found something personal to pick on about Harold's appearance.

'What sort o' 'Nancy-Boy' blouse do ee' be wearing as a public servant?' Miss Worsnip went on.

'That's enough of that nasty talk,' Celia said sharply to Miss Worsnip. She'd overheard the remark as she'd followed Miss Worsnip onto the van.

Celia winked at Harold. 'Morning Harold, did you manage to get that book I ordered?'

'Excuuuuuse me!' Miss Worsnip drew her angular body up into an exclamation mark, hands clasped together in front, elbows sticking out, sharp enough to poke a pig. 'I think you'm find that I was ere first!'

Betty Bins climbed into the van during the middle of this altercation.

'And,' continued Celia 'I think you'll find that the regulations state that council personnel must be treated with all due respect and courtesy, otherwise the facility provided, i.e. the Mobile Library will be withdrawn. I don't think the parishioners will thank you for being responsible for that Miss Worsnip, do you?'

Miss Worsnip, for once lost for words, left her returned books on the counter and hustled her way down to the other end of the library bus, taking a book off the shelf at random and pretending to read. Harold, Celia and Betty shared a smile and stifled their giggles as they saw the title of the book; 'Fifty Shades of Grey' and Harold started counting under his breath. 'One, two, thr... there she blows!'

Miss Worsnip thrust the book away from her and threw the words, 'disgusting filth,' at them all as she stomped down from the van.

All three attempted to control their laughter to levels not to be heard outside of the van as they didn't wish to embarrass the poor woman further.

'Do the regulations really say that Celia?' asked Harold.

'I haven't a clue, I've never read them but I expect so.' Celia replied with a chuckle.

Betty and Harold were cousins and Betty was very protective of Harold whom she knew to be one of the kindest men anyone could wish to find. Harold and Betty had swapped clothes from about the age of three. Having had a sensible mother he'd been allowed to wear what he wanted. Him and Betty were a similar size and would swap clothes all the time. Once he started school, Harold would go off to school wearing his school uniform quite happily, then when he arrived home he would change into whatever he wished. It hadn't been easy for Harold as he grew up but he knew he was always able to be himself in St Urith.

'By the way Harold, I think you look very smart, I love that shade of minky lilac and how lucky to find trousers that compliment it.'

'Thank you, Betty, you don't think the bird pattern too much?' Asked Harold.

'Absolutely not, it's a nice contrast to the plain trousers. If you find me a couple of books that you know Miss Worsnip will like I'll pop them around to her on my way home,' replied Betty.

'Will do Betty,' replied Harold as he took in her books and placed them on the returning shelf. This reminded Harold about the piece of paper left in the book that he was about to look at when Miss Worsnip arrived.

After Betty had gone on her way having chosen her books and two for Miss Worsnip, he picked up the book with the piece of paper edging out. It was a copy of 'Disappearing Houses of Devon', he pulled on the corner of the paper. Some random numbers, letters and measurements were written in blue ink. Looking at them, they didn't make any sense to Harold. Celia had chosen a book about patchwork to go with her ordered book on textile art and moved to the desk for Harold to check them out.

'Celia? What do you make of this? I found it in this book.' Harold held up the paper and book.

Celia took the piece of paper from Harold and looked at it, then at the book. 'I have a copy of that book Harold, it's out of print now but very interesting. I'm not sure what this is though, I mean I can see that it's measurements of something but not what the letters mean. If it was in this book I'm guessing that someone was researching something.' Celia passed the book and the piece of paper back and picked up her books.

'Who borrowed the book last?' asked Celia heading out the door.

'That new chap...Max something? Replied Harold.

Celia stopped and turned back towards Harold, 'Max Cheetham?' she asked.

'That's 'im'.

'Interesting... Perhaps he'll come back for it. I should hang on to it just in case Harold. Bye now, and thanks for the books.' Celia gave a small wave before stepping down from the van. It was only as she walked away she remembered that she had forgotten to ask Harold if he had seen Cat's van.

Harold's Tin

Harold had a small tin box that he kept all the bit and pieces that people left in books or on the shelves. Reaching under the counter he pulled the box out. Originally it had contained biscuits. It was square in shape and around the sides was a pattern of white and yellow daisies on a background of orange. On the top the background was bright yellow with large sunflowers and daisies, it was typical 1970's. The figures dominating the design were Harold's favourite, or rather the girl was, and what she was wearing. The girl's auburn hair was piled up on top of her head in large curls with stray tendrils lying on her neck and in front of her ears. The black scooped neck top with blue and purple flowers had a white scalloped collar and bell sleeves. Harold loved the full skirt with its multi coloured stripes of orange, pink and brown, supported he guessed by some stiff net petticoats.

Harold's interest in clothes had started when he

was a student in college because a lot of the students dressed themselves in all sorts of different costumes and styles and this gave Harold the freedom to wear what he wanted. It was then that he had started making his own clothes. He collected vintage fabrics and interesting clothes from jumble sales, to alter or remake into his own designs. On one such foray into a charity shop he had found the tin. Inside there was a selection of cottons, bits of lace, elastic and pins and needles. Harold had been thrilled.

Waving Celia goodbye Harold picked up the tin and looked down at the picture. One day he would make that skirt. He had almost everything he needed to recreate the outfit the girl on the tin was wearing. Opening the lid, he put the paper inside, closed it and tucked it away back under the counter. As he waited for his next customer he pulled out a book from his tote lying under the counter 'Cake Decorating for Beginners'. As he turned the pages he thought with pleasure about the evening ahead. It was a Wednesday and that meant cake making classes and tonight they were expanding their repertoire and moving into the world of patisserie. Whether this unstoppable feeling of excitement was purely for the cake making, or perhaps at the thought of spending time with Inspector Pratt, Harold neither knew nor cared.

Harold had been single since Vincent his Brazilian boyfriend had been deported. The police had discovered his visa had run out when they took statements from everybody when there had been a murder in the village. Harold and the Inspector had struck up a friendship over the complications of creating a Battenberg. After three weeks of shy looks and smiles from Harold, and blushing and harrumphing from the Inspector, plus the occasional accidental tingling touch when they both reached for an egg or the time when the Inspectors hand closed over Harold's as they reached for the bottle of Madagascan Vanilla essence at the same time. Harold smiled and turned to the page for creating roses out of icing.

Lilac Davenport

As a child, Lilac Davenport had promised herself that when she grew up she would marry and have a family of her own to love and cherish. She would spend hours drawing pictures of wedding and bridesmaid dresses. Growing up, her hopes of a fairytale wedding faded but she still kept those childish pictures stored in a shoebox in her wardrobe. Then she had met Nathan, 'The One'. After six months she went out and bought a big storage box with a romantic picture of cupids decorating the lid. Inside, she gathered a collection of glossy pictures of impossibly thin brides in impossibly expensive dresses, cut from bridal magazines. The box had filled up and the top now had to be forced on as she waited for Nathan to pop the question. The years went on and then in the week of her approaching fortieth birthday, one lunchtime she stepped out of her office into the sunshine and sat down on a bench to eat her sandwiches and read the local paper. By the end of her forty-five minute lunch break all her hopes and dreams would have shattered into jagged pieces.

S.U.L.C

❧

C elia was enjoying a rather ripe camembert on a French baguette whilst sitting on her patio enjoying the warm early Spring sunshine. Celia loved her garden. It was South facing, so enjoyed a lot of light and sunshine. Although there weren't many, Celia was enjoying the few early flowers in the garden. The heads of the daffodils nodding in the breeze and the orange and yellow striped tulips bold in the sunshine were a sign of spring and, hopefully, of more sunny days to come. She looked across the fields and up to the hill on the horizon, where her friend Lady Marigold lived. I'm sure she should have returned from her holiday by now but I haven't heard that she's back and she hasn't been in touch which is unusual, she thought.

Leaving thoughts of Lady Marigold, Celia ruminated on last night's particularly fraught meeting of the Village Book Club, which was a branch of S.U.L.C. the St Urith's Ladies Club. She was nearly drummed out for admitting to reading her books on her Kindle. She pointed out to the one or two shocked and disapproving faces that because the Kindle was backlit it meant that she could still read in bed without disturbing Ronald after he had put his light out.

Layla Laverne asserted, 'it's dangerous to read in bed on a tablet!'

Celia pointed out, 'it's only dangerous if I hit Ronald over the head with it to stop his snoring!'

Layla persisted in her persecution of technical devices saying, 'reading devices should be banned. People are dying because they are reading on their phones and tablets, and that's another thing, why call them tablets, tha'st very confusing for some old people.'

Celia was a little concerned about Layla's mortality at this point because her colour had risen alarmingly. She was also amused at the possibility of someone being unsure of which one to swallow a tablet or a tablet.

'We should all be reading books and magazines. Now there's an example, magazines! How can you read a magazine on a tablet? You couldn't do the crossword or cut out a recipe...'

Celia interrupted, as much as to give Layla a chance to breathe as anything else, 'I don't read many magazines Layla, I don't want to know what frozen dinner Peter Andre is recommending, or the next new Dr Mosley diet, or be told what I must wear this season? I mean, what's that all about? I don't want to know about the grandmother who slept with her grandson's girlfriend. And before you say anything, I know you write and contribute to some of those magazines Layla, but I don't want to read them! But even if I did I could still read them on my Kindle.' Celia drew a ragged breath.

'Well, really!' protested Layla, 'you've just picked on stuff that you don't like and although you say you don't want to read magazines Celia, I've seen you in Tesco's buying them!'

Celia was annoyed at having been caught out by the bloody annoying Layla but realised that she had been a trifle tetchy and unfair. 'Layla, I apologise, you are absolutely right. I do treat myself now and again to a knitting or sewing magazine. I overreacted. Of course, everybody should be able to read whatever magazine they like. To be honest I would still buy the odd Women's Weekly if it hadn't gone down the same route as the others, nothing but diets and celebrities.'

'Well, one only has to look at you to see you're not interested in diets!' retorted Layla.

Seeing Celia's face following Layla's cutting remark, and hoping to prevent a full-blown cat-fight, Aunty Pat stepped in with a proposal for the next month's book. There is a lot more to Aunty Pat than a lot of people assume when they look at her and see just another older lady.

Most people are unaware that Aunty Pat set out from Great Torrington for Greenham Common in the 1960's to protest against nuclear weapons. Unfortunately, she only made it as far as St Urith With Well.

She had set up her tent against the north wall of St Urith's church, underneath a stone carving of the Green Man. Luckily, her best friend Ruby Bins lived over the way at the bakery, so she didn't have to actually sleep in the tent. She would wait until it was dark in case any reporters or TV were watching her and then she would nip over to Ruby's and sleep on the sofa. After an early breakfast she would be sat in front of her tent on her brother's fishing stool, holding up a banner which read 'WOMEN'S PEASE CAMP'. Spelling wasn't her best subject at school. Aunty Pat managed three whole days and two nights before Miss Worsnip the churchwarden threatened to call the police and have her evicted. She said she couldn't stand the ululating. Aunty Pat thought that she was probably jealous as every afternoon Ruby had brought bread and buns from her bakery and 'Birdie' (Mrs Finch) would rattle along with her tea trolley. The ladies had a high old tea-time party amongst the gravestones, but that was the end of Aunty Pat's nuclear protest.

'Let's read this book next month,' Aunty Pat shouted excitedly holding up a book, 'it's called the Cowboy and the Thief.'

Eight pairs of eyes swiveled to see what she was holding aloft because everyone knew it could be absolutely anything. Aunty Pat didn't have the usual censorship button that most people have in their brains that sorts things out and indicates that something is unsuitable. Like, something you might share with your friends you wouldn't necessarily share with the vicar's wife. No, Aunty Pat was uncensored. The cover of the book sported a half-naked man wearing nothing but a black cowboy hat, a pair of cut-off jeans slung so low he almost needed a bikini wax, and sporting a tattoo of a cactus on his bicep that could have been mistaken for something else. There were general gasps, murmurings and giggles then Ruby Bins raised her voice over the excited babble saying, 'Great idea Aunty Pat (everyone called her Aunty Pat). Some of you can get the e-book from the library, some can get it on their thingamajigs and Aunty Pat will pass her copy onto me and so on. Now, let's all have some tea and biscuits.'

'Do you know who's bought Stonepark then?' Audrey Boy asked as she tried to save half of her dunked Garibaldi before it turned into floating flies in her tea.

'I heard it was a pop star,' responded Trixie Bell.

'Never!' asserted Birdie Finch,' it's a lottery winner, g'wan to be one o' they 'oliday cottages.'

'Some cottage. There must be at least seven bedrooms,' Celia chipped in.

'Well I spect you'm git them angers on if you'm won lottry,' answered Birdie.

'I wouldn't give ouse-room to angers on!' Aunty Pat said to everyone's murmured agreement, 'but I would give ouse-room to that gorgeous hunk that be lodgin in Unkempt Muff,' she giggled, 'I'd like to see 'im with nothing but a cowboy 'at on.'

'Who wouldn't?' agreed Audrey Boys, 'I caught a glimpse of him topless the other evening on my way back from WW and Oh my goodness, I've never seen bumps on a man like that before.'

'That's not on your way home Audrey, you naughty lady,' Celia said.

'No, but I walk Aunty Pat back to her car, don't I Aunty Pat?'

'That's true, she does Celia,' asserted Aunty Pat with a smirk.

'Yes, but why does Aunty Pat park her car near the Unfurled Moth instead of outside the parish hall, where we hold the S.U.L.C. meeting?' Celia asked, but then seeing the smirking ladies said, 'actually, forget I asked.'

'Why don't we ask 'im to come and give us a talk?' suggested Aunty Pat

'You don't know what he does, so what would you ask him to talk about?' asked Celia.

'Sex,' replied Aunty Pat, laughing.

'That's a good idea, you can ask him Celia,' agreed Audrey.

There were mixed comments of, 'Jolly good idea, hear hear, be a craack'.

'On no, if you want him to come you can ask him Aunty Pat, anyway, what would you ask him to give a talk about? Celia asked.

'I don't care what 'ee says, 'ee don' even ave to talk but t'wood be good if 'ee dressed like him on here,' Aunty Pat waved her book about with the half-naked cowboy. The ladies erupted into laughter.

When Celia arrived home, she logged into the

library and tried to download a copy of the Cowboy and the Thief. Unfortunately, someone had booked it out before her and she had to have the audio version. It would be fine as long as she used her earphones, she thought, as she wasn't sure Ronald would be up to hearing erotic fiction whilst he was lying in bed reading his David Baldacci. Bleating from the newborn lambs in the field brought Celia back to earth. They were only a couple of hours old and the dear little things put a smile on her face. When just a few days old they would form little gangs and race and chase about the field, they were really comical. Sometimes they would try to suckle off a different mother and get pushed away roughly, she supposed that even they had trouble telling the sheep apart. Biting into her baguette loaded with cheese and tomatoes, a vicious piece of crust assaulted her gum, 'ouch!' After exploring with a finger, Celia deduced by the smear of blood that it was just a cut, nothing that a quick swill of wine couldn't deal with. The following night she used her electric toothbrush as usual but when she ventured to the sensitive area, she switched to a soft manual toothbrush. Ping! A lump of shrapnel hit the roof of her mouth, bounced off her tongue and dropped into the washbasin with a chink. F...ish!

Ronald Goes Shopping

First thing Monday morning Celia reluctantly phoned the dentist.

'So, it's just a filling is it Mrs Ladygarden?' the receptionist said.

'What do you mean just a filling?' responded Celia, 'a little more sympathy please!'

Celia's dentist was a jovial man and after the preliminary greetings he settled her into the dreaded chair and pulled up his mask.

'Right let's see what's going on,' he said and then without so much as a 'brace yourself', he reached in and snapped off half of her tooth. 'You didn't need that,' he said as he pulled his mask down and smiled at Celia's shocked face.

Celia had not been amused as she'd walked back to her car contemplating the thought of two further appointments. Posts and caps had been mentioned. She had just arrived at her car and reached out for the door handle, when a small pure white feather fluttered down and landed in her upturned palm.

After the dentist, Celia and Ronald drove into the center of Barnstaple as she wanted a few things from a well-known chain of chemists. Ronald is to shopping as Celia is to the dentist, so the minute they were through the doors he was off. Celia found it was better to let him go, then she could concentrate on her intended purchases. Celia was queuing at the counter when an overpowering fragrance arrived followed by Ronald, who was rubbing his chin.

'Feel that, bet you'd like some of that wouldn't you?' he said.

Celia, who had made it to the counter, wasn't sure who was the most embarrassed, her or the young assistant. She decided the best ploy would be to ignore him and carry on, so she handed her basket over but Ronald grabbed her hand and stroked his cheek with it.

'Feel that, I've just had a shave, they've got some fancy electric razors here, what do you think? Oh, and I put some of that Guvchy stuff on.'

Speechless, Celia hunted for her loyalty card, paid, and tried to leave as quickly as possible whilst trying not to look like a shoplifter, which was more likely to happen now there were no bags. She ended up clutching her purchases in her hands. Juggling her purse and her purchases, she made for the door leaving Ronald to trail behind wrestling the pink shopping bag with Porto written across it off his shoulder. As she neared the automatic doors, Ronald trailing behind, she was suddenly confronted by an over made up young woman with Frida Kahlo eyebrows proffering a perfume.

'Would you like to try this Angel Eau de Parfum or Angel Hair Mist? It's on special offer today and double points on your store card.'

'I'm sorry, I can't stop, he needs the toilet,' Celia replied grabbing hold of Ronald and herding him through the door.

Lilac's Nasty Surprise

L ilac was sitting on her favourite bench in the square in front of Barnstaple library, in the week of her approaching 40th birthday. To her right was the 11th century Motte, all that remained of Henry de Tracey's castle. She was interested in local history and had taken the time to learn a little about North Devon. The Motte was a bit battered now with well-worn pathways that children had made as they chased around the mound lost in their make-believe games. If the weather was reasonable she would usually sit and have her lunch here or down by the river Taw. Whilst she was munching on her homemade egg sandwich, she was thinking about how much she and her friend Rosie had enjoyed the outdoor performance of John Gay's 'The Beggar's Opera' they'd been to see at Rosemoor Gardens at the weekend. It was brilliant and such a treat to watch it in the setting of the beautiful gardens. The next rainy lunch-break she had to spend in the library, she would see what more she could find out about John Gay. She thought he had something to do with the Queens theatre but she wasn't sure.

Lilac finished eating, folded up the used bit of tin foil, and stuffed it inside her sandwich box. She couldn't abide litter. Unfortunately, the sandwich box had been holding down the local newspaper and as she picked it up the paper was lifted by a gust of wind. She snatched at the pages as they fanned out and flew up into the air and across the square. She felt an idiot chasing them about. Every time she reached a piece, it blew a few steps further on. It was the paper equivalent of Grandma's footsteps. Catching the eye of a woman who was attempting to stop the wind blowing her skirt up, they shared a smile as she managed to grab the bulk of it before it blew all over the square. The once slim paper felt twice the size as she shuffled the pages about and attempted to fold it back into a manageable size. As she pushed the paper down into her tote a face as familiar as her own grinned out at her from the printed page.

It was Nathan. Hands shaking, she slowly pulled the newspaper out and smoothed it flat, not taking her eyes off the picture. She read it twice just to make sure she hadn't misunderstood. It was the sports section of the newspaper. She read the caption and discovered it was a picture of Nathan and his 'wife' holding aloft a silver trophy, their prize for winning a mixed doubles skittles tournament in Crediton. Lilac Davenport walked back to work in shock, not really looking where she was going. As she went through the door to the records office she bumped into a man, scattering the papers he had obviously been clutching.

Monty Butler hastily stuffed the papers back into the envelope marked 'Stonepark' Max had asked him to collect from the records office. He frowned as caught sight of the words 'National Heritage List' but then Lilac spoke, interrupting his thoughts and making him forget everything - including how to talk it seemed.

'Sorry,' Lilac muttered automatically.

'Hi... sorry... hi...' Monty looked up into Lilac's eyes, the beautiful woman he had picked up (literally!) last year. 'Hey, are you OK?' he asked, flustered, as he stood up.

Lilac looked up at him. The deep brown voice had come from a man she had seen quite a few times in the village. He'd also helped her up once when she tripped and fell down the path at her bungalow, but she couldn't remember his name.

'I don't know if you remember me, my name's Monty, Monty Butler. I live in the same village as you.' Monty, normally a confident person, felt like a teenager in Lilac's presence.

'Are you OK? You look as white as a sheet,' Monty said.

'Yes thanks, I'm fine, I've got to get back to work,' Lilac pushed past him and went back to her office leaving Monty to gaze after her.

Where's the Little Woman?

※❀❀

Sir Reginald Knowles made his way into the breakfast room and sat down in his customary chair at the head of the table. He wrinkled his nose at the sight and smell of yesterday's breakfast - the greasy remains of egg and bacon, a marmalade jar with the butter knife protruding from the top and two pieces of toast at rest in the silver toast rack. Looking at the toast rack, he idly wondered where the matching silver coaster that the marmalade usually rested on had gone. It wasn't long before Mrs Budgen, the housekeeper at Copshott Hall, pushed and hip-punched the door open where it rebounded off the same dent in the plaster wall that it did every morning. She plonked the heavy tray down on the opposite end of the long mahogany table from where Sir Reginald sat. Picking up a plate containing a full English breakfast of bacon, sausage, eggs, tomatoes and black pudding, she walked the length of the table and plonked it down again, in front of Sir Reginald. Mrs Budgen was an expert at plonking. She shuffled back for the teapot, cup and saucer, back and forth, until the tray was empty. Shuffling her way around to the other side of the table she started her dosy-doe back and forth to the tray with yesterday's used crockery and redundant tea paraphernalia. Although he was used to this daily assault on his senses, he still couldn't control his start at every scrape, crash, clatter and bang.

Sir Reginald still hadn't realised his wife hadn't returned from her holiday. He was vague about dates and times unless it was a meet marked on the racing calendar. A letter from the travel company had been sent regretfully informing Sir Reginald that his wife had gone missing in the desert, and despite several extensive searches she had not been found. He hadn't opened the letter, or read it. He had assumed it was marketing rubbish so ripped it in half and threw it in his wastepaper bin with the rest of the junk mail. On this particular morning he looked around the breakfast table almost expecting to see 'good old Marigold' there, but all he saw was her chair pushed back from the table as if she had just arisen. He wasn't unduly concerned. He picked up a large brown envelope which had been waiting for him with the rest of the post when he'd arrived at the breakfast table. As usual, it had already been opened.

'Blast the woman,' he muttered.

Mrs Budgen was an inveterate snoop and it didn't matter how many times he told her that he would sack her if she didn't stop opening his mail, she still did it. In Sir Reginald's long years of experience nothing good ever arrived in a brown envelope and one should avoid them at all costs. This was an especially large envelope and he suddenly felt rather nervous as to what it might contain so decided to ignore it and tucked into his breakfast and morning paper. When he'd finished eating he folded his paper up neatly, revealing the brown envelope lying underneath it stark against the white damask cloth. Automatically, he pushed it across to Marigold's place as he rose from his chair. She always dealt with the paperwork, she could sort it. Then, as he looked at the empty space he remembered that she wasn't there. Annoyed, he sat back down and pulled the envelope towards him, reaching reluctantly inside for the contents. The first thing he pulled out was a letter from Marigold.

Dear Reginald,

You may or may not have noticed that I have not returned from my holiday in Africa (probably not!) I won't beat about the bush (which is funny, considering where I'm living). I want a divorce and the relevant papers are enclosed. Please, for both our sakes, sign them at once and return them to my solicitors in the enclosed stamped addressed envelope. If the stamped addressed envelope is not there then Mrs Budgen will have taken it (look in the bread bin in the kitchen if she won't fess up.)

Please don't think of refusing to sign or I will be forced to go down the messy route of citing your many dalliances over the years and naming names (which could be embarrassing for yourself and the Royal Family.)

I have written separately to Sharon and she will deal with my personal effects as per my instructions. I am selling Stonepark and the agents have the keys, so you shouldn't have to do anything. The owners will be calling for the set of keys in the box in the hall. I would be grateful if you would pass them over. I have sorted out all the rest of my affairs in England so there shouldn't be anything outstanding, but if there is, or any further correspondence, I would be grateful if you could send it to my solicitors.

I wish you all the best with the rest of your life, Reginald.

Marigold

HE LAID the letter down amongst the scattering of toast crumbs and salt and pepper and slowly picked up his copy of Sporting Life staring at it unseeingly.

The Handover

Max Cheetham was nervous. His hands were trembling slightly as one rested on the papers in his man bag, the other raised to the large iron knocker. Once he'd taken this next step there would be no turning back. He would be committed to carrying it through. Hesitating, he considered the options but quickly discounted all thoughts of pulling out, and knocked on the door of Copshott Hall. He was beginning to think that nobody was going to answer but eventually the weather-beaten oak door creaked open and a dazed looking man with receding hair moved into the doorway. The man was wearing a worn tweed jacket over a green checked shirt and green wool tie. Little did Max know how lucky he was to catch Sir Reginald at his most vulnerable on this particular morning. Sir Reginald couldn't even remember the journey from the breakfast room to the front door. He couldn't even explain why he opened the front door, it was Mrs Budgen's job. Max, usually smooth tongued and ready for anything, paused. He hadn't expected Sir Reginald himself to answer the door and he had been prepared to cajole the housekeeper with a well-practiced speech.

'Alright, I know what you're after!' barked Sir Reginald.

Max stepped back nervously but to his surprise Sir Reginald turned to a console table at the side of the hall on which sat a magnificent English Regency Chinoiseries decorated box that Max would have given his right arm for. Sir Reginald unlocked and opened the box and took out a heavy ornate key and several other keys, handed them to him and closed the door before Max had even uttered a word. Max looked down at the keys in his hand labelled Stonepark written in black ink and couldn't believe his luck. He'd been hoping to smooth talk his way into borrowing the keys as the sale hadn't quite completed and the agents wouldn't release them until all monies had been transferred. If he could get in there, he could get a head start before Monty and his team arrived.

Lilac Takes Action

Home from work, and on her second glass of wine, Lilac felt shocked and humiliated. Nathan was married! It didn't matter how many times she kept saying it, it still seemed impossible. Although her relationship with Nathan hadn't been perfect (whose was?) she was still finding it difficult to believe what she had read in the paper that lunchtime. How could she have been so stupid, so easily taken in, how could he be married? Why had she accepted and believed all his lies? The whole relationship was based on a lie. Nathan was a milkman from Crediton and she had waited years for him to ask her to marry him. There had been times when she had thought he was going to but it had never happened. He wouldn't even move in permanently, there was always an excuse and now that made sense. Nathan's clothes were in his wardrobe in their bedroom, his toiletries in the bathroom. For God's sake he stayed over twice a week and they had been on holiday together for one week every year. How did he explain that to his wife? She asked herself. She asked herself how in Devon had he managed to keep his two lives separate all this time? It was a flippin' miracle considering everyone knew everyone else in a thirty mile radius.

Lilac was resourceful and strong, she'd had to be. She had no family to support her and only a few friends. Not that she wasn't sociable, she was, but Nathan worked long hours and in between he was at evening college studying- or so he had said. She supposed that was a lie too. Most of their arguments were about her having to go out on her own all the time. Thinking about it now, it was all beginning to make sense. He probably isn't studying at college, that was an excuse for him not to spend more time with her. Probably doesn't even live with his mother, the bastard. What an idiot she had been. What a bastard he was. She felt sick with loss. The loss of the life she thought she had, and the loss of the life she hoped to have had. Not forgetting the free milk and clotted cream every week that went on the homemade scones she baked for him, the bastard. She was angry. So angry she could kill. She wanted to break things, scream at the top of her voice, tear her hair out. But how do you do all that with the eyes of the world on you? You only have to sneeze in a small village like St Urith With Well for someone to knock on the door with a box of tissues.

This crisis with Nathan the Bastard, as she had now renamed him, had also come at a time when there was uncertainty at work. Lilac had started working in the Records Office straight from college, which she had left with one respectable A level in English Literature and a diploma in cake decorating. If Lilac could have picked the perfect job then hers was it and she loved it. However, in the slipstream of government cuts, the records office in Barnstaple was to be closed and moved to Plymouth. When she had told Nathan the Bastard he had told her in no uncertain terms that he wouldn't move to Plymouth. Then she remembered what else he'd said, 'but I thought you wanted to get married in St Urith's church?' The bastard, she thought, the full knowledge of his betrayal and web of lies weighing on her like a full metal jacket.

With Nathan the Bastard out of the picture she could if she wanted move to Plymouth, keep her job and start afresh where nobody would know of her humiliation. In her heart even though, she knew the gossips would wear their tongues out talking about her and she didn't want to leave the village. She had come to love St Urith's for its quietness and friendliness. She even enjoyed the twelve mile drive to work every day through the beautiful North Devon Countryside. The colour of the trees, fields and hedgerows were ever changing through the seasons, from lemon green in Spring through to the Autumn ochres, reds and golds, there was even the occasional sparkling blue glimpse of the sea. Living in her bungalow she had never felt alone even though Nathan the Bastard had only stayed over two nights a week. It was small but perfect in her eyes.

Thank goodness, she hadn't given in to Nathan the Bastard who'd wanted her to add his name to the deeds! Where would that have left her now? There were only two bedrooms, but they were a good size, and her favourite room the sitting room had an ever-changing view over parkland where sheep and horses grazed.

She cried almost nonstop for what felt like three weeks but in reality, was only three days, then decided enough was enough. Telephoning the Records office, she told them her stomach upset had gone and she would return the following morning. Her boss tantalisingly told her that she had some news for her, but wouldn't say what it was over the phone, she would see her in the morning. Switching her mobile off, her tongue was itching. What did that mean? Was it like itchy palms, with money going out if it was your right hand and coming in if it was your left hand? Lilac walked to the corner of her sitting room where her writing bureau stood with a printer on a small table next to it. She took a fresh piece from a packet of printing paper and grabbed a pen out of a cubbyhole. Sitting in her favourite armchair by the picture window she started writing.

1. Tell Nathan the Bastard never to contact her again in any lifetime

2. Visit the dog rescue center and get herself a dog

3. Negotiate part-time hours at work. If office moves to Plymouth then find a new job

4. Set up her own online bespoke Cake Decorating business

6. Enter into village life - join clubs.

READING over what she had written Lilac felt a frisson of excitement and a flicker of hope. There was no way she was going to waste any more of her life waiting for a knight in shining armour to appear. Not that she would turn one down if he came knocking on her door. She had no idea why but a picture of a certain handsome guy with a cheeky smile popped into her head.

Laying the list down on the arm of the chair she wished she had a mum she could call and talk it over with, rant and rave too. Lilac couldn't remember her own mother. She'd read somewhere that some people have a memory of a certain smell or a song or bits of a story from their mothers. Lilac wasn't sure she believed it, she thought that it was more likely people wanting to have a memory of their mothers. Or perhaps she just didn't allow herself to remember anything because it was too painful. Lilac's first memories were of bouncing between care home and foster homes. Then she was placed in what was meant to be a long-term foster home. It hadn't started well, she had been a difficult little girl, but it didn't seem to matter what she did, Nancy and David would just calmly clear up whatever mess she had made or sort out any problems with never a harsh word. Eventually she had come to realise that she was safe and she could stay there, and most important of all, that she was loved. Nancy and David had wanted to adopt her. One glorious day, they had sat her down and explained everything and asked her if she would like to be their real daughter and stay with them forever. It never happened. It wasn't until she was officially an adult and was able to obtain a copy of her file from social services that she found out that her birth mother had refused to sign the papers relinquishing the rights to Lilac.

When she was sixteen, Nancy and David were on their way home from a concert in heavy rain and as they were driving around a sharp bend the car aquaplaned David lost control and sadly they both died. Lilac was put into a one room bedsitter in a women's refuge in Exeter and given a business card with a social worker's number on it. Life was not good. When Lilac was eighteen, to her surprise, she inherited a legacy from Wendy and David. Some of it she used to travel and when she'd had enough of that and wanted to put down the roots she had never had, she bought her bungalow. They were the best of parents for the short time she had them, and she only wished they were still with her. She would be forever grateful to them. She knew that just as she had all those years ago, she must start her life over again. This time it would be different. This time she had the security of her own home, a car and a job, well perhaps her job wasn't the most secure at the moment, but she had a future to look forward to. And it wouldn't include Nathan the Bastard. She would never put her life in the hands of someone else again.

Back at work the next day meeting her boss over a

cup of coffee she was informed that due to over-whelming public protest the Record Office would remain in Barnstaple. Whilst her boss was happy with the good news, Lilac took the opportunity to request shorter hours. This didn't seem to be a problem, in fact, her boss thought that the powers that be would be happy to save some money on her reduced wages. In her lunch break she searched the local Petroc college's website until she found what she was looking for. 'Cake Decorating Classes' twelve week course on Tuesday and Thursday evenings 6 - 9pm'. She immediately enrolled online and paid her fee, wincing a little at the cost.

At home that evening she sat and read the course details she had printed off on her printer, along with a list of items needed for the course. A lot of things she already had but she looked forward to a bit of retail therapy which always cheered her up. The course was just what she needed to brush up and update her cake decorating skills and it was due to start after Easter, which was in two weeks time, so she didn't have long to wait. Having put into motion number 3 and 4 on her list, she felt able to tackle number 1: Getting rid of Nathan the Bastard. He was coming around tonight as was usual on a Wednesday because it was his Mother's Bingo night, or that's what she had been led to believe. Now there was a possibility that for 'mother' read 'wife'. Laying the course details down onto the coffee table she went into the kitchen. She still took pleasure in its pale blue glossy cupboards and polished concrete worktops. Reaching into the cupboard under the sink, she took out a roll of black plastic rubbish sacks and walked purposefully into her bedroom. First, she emptied the chest of drawers from his side of the bed, it all went into two sacks. There was a new box of condoms which she opened and pulled out one at a time then stuffed them in between the socks, boxers and t-shirts. Ripping two more sacks off the roll, she opened the small wardrobe that Nathan the Bastard used, joggers, jeans and jumpers filled the first bag, jackets and trousers the other.

In the bathroom she gathered his razors, shaving cream, aftershave, moisturisers, hair putty, shower gel and deodorant, thinking, lord he's got more smellies than me! She refrained from doing the expected of emptying the contents of the bottles over his clothes but did enjoy just chucking them on top. After tying them up she carried them out two at a time and placed them on the side of the driveway. In the garage she picked up the cat carrier and after glancing around to make sure there wasn't anything else she went out by the courtesy door locking it behind her.

In the kitchen she scooped up the unsuspecting cat from where it was enjoying a catnap in the hanging bed attached to the radiator and put it gently into the cat container.

'Sorry puss, but I didn't want a cat, I've always wanted a dog and you're really Nathan the Bastard's cat, so you can go and live with him and his wife.'

Unhooking the cat bed, she laid it on the kitchen

floor and filled it with cat food, cat biscuits, a toy mouse, a feather thing on a stick and two cat bowls. Picking this up and tucking it under her arm she reached for the cat container carrying it all out to join the dustbin bags on the driveway. It wasn't raining so the cat would be fine she thought. Finally, she scanned the picture of Nathan the Bastard and his wife from the newspaper, enlarged and printed it, and slipped it into a plastic sleeve. She walked back out to the drive and taped the picture to the top of the cat container from which a pitiful howling was now coming. As she straightened up a voice called out,

'You alright gal?'

Looking out to the road to where the voice came from, she saw the good-looking guy she'd bumped into at work the other day, the same guy who'd popped into her head the other day. She knew he had told her his name but for the life of her she couldn't remember it. She had often seen him walking past her bungalow and had enjoyed a quick look – well, what red-blooded woman wouldn't? He was a well-built, good-looking guy. Last year he had been passing her bungalow when she had stupidly fallen over and he'd helped her to her feet. When he pulled her up, she'd grabbed hold of his arm and had felt the solid muscle on muscle. At the time, she couldn't help comparing him to Nathan. Realising the guy was still waiting for an answer she called back, 'Yes, fine thank you.'

'Do you need an and wiv that lot bird?' Monty

asked, as he bent down to open the metal gate that secured the drive.

Lilac put her hand up like a French gendarme stopping the traffic 'No, no. I've finished now er... I'm really sorry but I've forgotten your name.'

'Monty love. Well if yer sure. I'll see you again,' he said, then waved and walked on.

She was just able to get back inside and bolt the front door as Nathan the Bastard pulled up outside the gate. Standing back from the window in the spare room that looked over the driveway she could see without being seen as Nathan the Bastard stepped out of his car. She watched him pause as he noticed the cat carrier and dustbin bags on the drive. Opening the gate, he walked to the cat carrier and squatted down, puzzlement skewing his face. She saw him rip off the plastic covered newspaper copy, pull out the picture, screw it into a ball and throw it down angrily. He was banging on the front door and holding his finger down on the bell. When it didn't open he started shouting through the letterbox. When that didn't bring her to the door he banged on the windows shouting, 'let me in Lilac, I can explain!'

Lilac stood impassively in the shadows.

Monty Butler

＊＊＊

Monty Butler was a bachelor. Not from choice, he loved women, he just hadn't met the right woman. That is until he set his eyes on Lilac Davenport. When he moved to Devon temporarily, Monty had not been expecting or prepared to fall in love. Always successful with women, and happy to be footloose and fancy free, when he fell for Lilac Davenport it was hard, fast and set to last. Monty had moved into a room above the Unfurled Moth public house in St Urith's, pleasing Fred the landlord who was struggling to keep the pub open. The room and position was perfect for Monty who kept himself to himself and would disappear for a couple of days every now and then. When the nosier of the pub's clientele asked where Monty had come from and what was he doing here in St Urith, Fred Dimmock the landlord replied,

'Dunno, don' care, ee' pays ees' rent, that's all I need to know.'

This annoyed everyone no end because usually Fred was always happy to put his two penn'orth in when it wasn't asked for. A short time after his arrival, Monty had become occasional drinking partners with Max Cheetham, another relatively newcomer to the village. It was perhaps inevitable that they should strike up a friendship, but it seemed as if this was restricted to the Unfurled Moth. In fact, appearances were deceptive as Monty and Max had met earlier in the year.

Max had put the word out in certain circles that he was looking for an expert for a project that he had planned in North Devon. Monty had contacted Max as being interested and he had sent over by courier details of the project. Monty had made a whistle stop trip to North Devon to recce the area and the outside of the property. That trip was to change Monty's life because on a walk around the village near to the property he would be working on, he met Lilac. Monty arranged to meet Max in the Thomas a Becket public house in the Old Kent Road in London. It had been a haunt of Monty's for some years due to its association with the boxing world. An amateur boxer in his youth, Monty would sit over his pint and imagine Henry Cooper training upstairs on the first floor. Legend has it that two of his heroes Muhammed Ali and Joe Frazier had dropped in for a spot of sparring. The Thomas a Becket was also famous for being the rehearsal space for David Bowie in the 70s when he wrote 'The Rise and Fall of Ziggy Stardust' and 'Spiders from Mars' album.

'I'll get my lot in as soon as you give me the word,' said Monty, looking at Max over his pint.

'Bit of a change of plan there, old chap, the client still wants you and your expertise, he wants you to do the work but he wants to use his own men to assist you,' Max replied.

'No way Jose, this job requires experts that's why you're employing me. I only work with my own crew and what about my insurance? It only covers me and my men,' asserted Monty.

'Listen Monty, this client doesn't mess about. He always gets what he wants and I'm certainly not brave enough to gainsay him.'

'You might not be, but I'm happy to stand up to whoever it is. I only work with my own people. It's skilled work, we're not cowboy builders you know. I don't have to take this job, I get plenty of work,' Monty responded angrily.

'Of course, I don't think you are a cowboy builder Monty, your reputation as an architectural salvager is outstanding, that's why we wanted you for this job. I quite understand how you feel but listen,' Max leaned towards Monty conspiratorially, 'look this is in total confidence, this client is a Russian Oligarch and I'm sorry, but if you decide to take on the job whatever conditions he lays down will have to be complied with,' Max said.

'What about a compromise Max? Me and my team will do the actual cutting away of the pieces and the fitting of the replacements and the Russian's men can do the loading and taking away. Have a word with your Oligarch, tell him if he wants to guarantee that the pieces remain intact and in perfect condition, he'd do best by letting us do it. If not, he can find someone else. Oh, and I still want the same money for the job. I'll get us another drink while you get on the dog and bone,' Monty said. He turned his back on Max and picked up his glass.

'OK Monty you win, he's agreed to your terms and you'll still get paid the same but the client wants his men on site all the time. They won't interfere with the job but he wants them there for security, so you can't lose, what do you say? Are you in or are you out?' Max asked.

Monty picked up his pint and took a mouthful to give himself time to think. He'd travelled all over the country with his business but he had never had cause to visit North Devon before. But how glad he was that he had because he had met the gorgeous Lilac and he didn't want to lose the chance of going back to St Urith where he hoped to ask her out. The girl had somehow got under his skin and he hadn't been able to forget her.

'Ok, you're right, I can't really lose, and bit of fresh country air will do me good, put roses in me cheeks won't it?' Monty laughed.

'Yes, quite. But you'll need to be discreet. No driving through the village, or everyone will know before you've driven out the other side. I've never known a place like it, they make MI6 look slack,' said Max.

'Don't worry about that, discreet is my middle name. I've sussed out how the land lies and I've found a way in that doesn't go near the village. Took me a while though, bloody hell there's a lot of lanes! They twist and twirl, some of em has grass down the middle for Christ's sake! And you can't see where you're going, the banks is as high as an 'ouse, then you find you're going the opposite direction to the one you want! I've never known a place like it!' exclaimed Monty.

'Are you sure you can get a lorry in that way?' asked Max.

'A lorry? Naah, never get a lorry through there. No, I'm using my noddle aren't I?' smiled Monty, tapping an index finger against his temple.

'What make is that? I've never heard of a Noddle. Stupid the names they keep calling cars, anyway it doesn't matter as long as it's big enough and I presume you have checked that?' asked Max.

Monty roared with laughter, 'Cor, you are a laugh Max and no mistake!'

Max was not amused and Monty, realising that he hadn't seen the joke. and wasn't one to be made a fool of, jumped in quick to make amends.

'It's OK mate, it's a large van and there's plenty of room, easier to get around the lanes and less conspicuous.

Max's proposal had come just at the right time for Monty. He was basically an honest man, and proud of his work, but he had unintentionally become involved in something that was a bit too sticky for his tastes.

Breaking the contract, he decided he could do with getting out of London for a while as the people who had paid for his services weren't too happy. It was just as well that he didn't know that something stickier would await him in deepest darkest Devonshire.

Garden Angel

❧❦❧

Celia couldn't say why she bought it. They'd gone up to the Recycling Centre looking for a slimline water-butt but there wasn't one. They'd found plenty of pots, but as she had brought some up to recycle she wasn't interested. She was trying, and failing, to persuade Ronald that a composter was a good idea when out of the corner of her eye she saw a flash. Drawn like a magpie to a shiny object, Celia abandoned the composter and went to see what it was whilst Ronald went to dump some old pots and bits of old wood and then wait in the car. It was a shiny aluminum ball on a thin rod, which Celia presumed pushed into the ground, and on the top was an angel. Without thinking too much about it, she picked it up and went to the office in the metal container.

'Hiya,' Celia said to the woman who was manning the Centre that day.

'Hi, how are you?'

'Fine thanks, You?'

'Yep, you want that?'

'Yes please, how much?' Celia held the garden ornament up.

'A pound OK?' the woman replied.

'Perfect,' Celia paid the money and walked back to the car.

'What on earth have you got there?' demanded Ronald.

'It's for the garden,' replied Celia, tucking it down on the floor carefully.

'Bit tacky, isn't it?' asked Ronald, 'I thought we were bringing rubbish to the dump, not buying it to take home.'

'Well, it might look tacky now but when it's in the garden amongst the greenery and flowers it will catch the light and look great,' Celia shot back snippily.

Ronald rolled his eyes, but decided it would be safer not to say anything more.

They drove down the winding lane into the village in silence because Celia was miffed with Ronald. They could see Dartmoor in all its splendour in the distance. Today, although you could see it reasonably well, there was a slight haze but that was OK because there is a local saying 'Dartmoor clear, rain is near.' As they drove into the village Celia noticed Max and Monty in conflab outside the Unfurled Moth. Celia saw Monty pull a large envelope from inside his jacket and passed it to Max who hurriedly pushed it into his bag.

'Ronald, stop the car!' Celia shouted.

Ronald slammed his feet on the brakes and they screeched to a stop.

'What the hell? What is it Celia? I didn't see anything, is it a cat? asked Ronald.

'No, I'll walk home from here,' Celia replied.

'What on earth for? We're nearly home now,' said Ronald irritated.

'I need to speak to those chaps, I'll only be five minutes,' Celia said.

'Celia, you're mad, you make me do an emergency stop for nothing and now you want to talk to people you don't even know!'

'Ronald there's something going on with these two,' Celia said.

'Look, I know you're curious, but you can't just go up to strangers and start interrogating them. I know you think you are a detective after what happened last year but you're not, and quite honestly, I can't go through that again, I thought I'd lost you.'

'It's nothing like last time Ronald. Nobody has been murdered, and anyway, I'm not going to interrogate them, I'm just going to chat to them,' Celia replied getting out of the car.

'OK, you know best, but be careful, and if you are not home in fifteen minutes I'm coming to find you.' Poor devils don't stand a chance Ronald said to himself as he drove off.

Celia on the Case

'Hi, I hope you don't mind me interrupting but I thought I'd come and introduce myself, I'm Celia Ladygarden.'

Monty was the first to recover.

'Ello love, I'm Monty,' Monty gave Celia one of his dazzling smiles.

'And I'm Max, how do you do Celia? Delighted to meet you,' Max held out his hand but it hung in mid-air as Celia still had her eyes firmly fixed on Monty.

'Fishing Hell! I see what the ladies mean now,' she said, as she couldn't help but look at all the important bits of Monty which were revealed by his tight fitting pale blue linen trousers and tight white T-shirt. Starting at his muscular thighs, her next stop was his satisfying man-bulge before she tore her eyes away and crept up his spectacular chest and only just stopped herself from running her hand up and down the impressive muscles of his arms.

'Hello Monty,' Celia smiled back, 'I thought I would say hello as I was passing, haven't had a chance before.'

Celia shook Max's hand, and as he reached out to her she caught sight of a glossy antiques catalogue poking out of his bag. Max, following Celia's gaze, dropped his hand quickly and poked the book back into his man bag.

'What are you young men cooking up then? I've seen you in conflab a couple of times lately, not up to anything you shouldn't be I hope?' Celia asked.

Both men looked taken aback. Monty looked at Max to come up with an answer who immediately moved into slick mode.

'My dear Celia, I do believe I've heard all about you,' he turned and looked meaningfully at Monty who picked up on the silent signal and excused himself.

'Sorry love, gotta go, nice to meet yer though,' Monty saluted Celia and ducked inside the Unfurled Moth.

'Now, am I right? You are the young lady who writes the village pantomimes?' Max said.

'You are half right. I am the woman who writes the village pantomime,' Celia replied. Young lady indeed, he's made a mistake if he thinks he can flatter me with cheesy flattery, thought Celia.

'Hmm yes quite, well erm... I've heard great things about it.' Max said slightly flustered, but trying to keep it together.

'And what exactly is your line of work, Max?' Celia

asked, looking Max in the eyes with the piercing binocular stare of a Buzzard.

'Oh well, you know, I keep busy,' Max replied, backing away from Celia's raptor gaze.

'I'm sure you do, but what do you keep busy at Max?' Celia persisted, stepping forward into his space.

'Well, it was supposed to be a secret but I'm sure you will keep it to yourself Celia. I'm writing a book and I thought what better place than the peace and quiet of North Devon.'

'And what about Mr Monty, is he writing a book too?' Celia asked

God this woman is a nightmare, thought Max, does she never give up? 'I don't think so that would be too much of a coincidence, no we just enjoy a pint together occasionally. Now if you excuse me I must get back to my writing.' Max turned to go.

'I'll walk with you as far as my road,' Celia turned to walk alongside Max. Convinced the man was lying, she persisted in her questioning. 'Am I allowed to know what the book is about, as a fellow writer?

'Am I allowed to know what the next pantomime is going to be?' asked Max smiling.

'Absolutely not. Nobody ever knows until we have our first read through,' Celia replied.

'Then you understand that I can't tell you what my book is about. Bye Celia, nice to have met you.' Max left Celia standing at the end of her road. Checkmate he thought to himself as he walked on.

Celia was absolutely fuming as she walked up the

road towards home. Smarmy bugger, she thought. You are definitely up to no good, and I will find out what you are up to, I will.

Ronald made Celia a cup of tea as soon as she walked through the front door, but of course she had to greet the fur babies first. You would have thought she had been away for days instead of an hour at the fuss they made. Little Polly was padding her front paws up and down in between rubbing her face up and down on Celia's legs, whilst Hirsute Roley was jumping up and down and talking away in his own little doggy language. Ronald was just taking the teabag out as Celia made it to the kitchen.

'Well, found out everything? What size shoes they wear, their inside leg measurement?' Ronald asked.

'Ha, ha very funny. No, but that Max is up to something I know it, he's a real smarmy con-man type but the other, Monty he's called, he's a different kettle of fish. I get a completely different feeling about him than I do about that Max character, he couldn't get away from me fast enough,' Celia replied

'Quite a few people try and do that when they meet you Celia, especially coming up to panto time,' Ronald chuckled.

'That's different and you know it. No, I believe Monty to be an honest person and I think he rushed away because he obviously is tied in with that Max character and was frightened of saying something that might give away what they are up to. What's more I think I might know what that might be, I've just remembered something I saw on Facebook about robberies in some of the big houses in the area, hang on.' Celia went to fetch her iPad which she switched on and started searching.

'Here's your tea, don't let it get cold, you know what you're like once you get on that thing, you'll be on it for hours,' Ronald said.

'No, I won't, I'm just trying to find the bit on the police website about these thefts. Ah here it is.' Celia read some of the article to Ronald. 'Small but extremely valuable items have been stolen from several National Trust properties in the South West over the past few weeks. I bet it's that Max and Monty,' Celia asserted.

'Celia, you don't know that, you can't go around accusing people of theft!'

'Ronald, I haven't accused anybody yet! But I think they're involved and I'm going to prove it.'

'No Celia, remember what happened last time you became embroiled in crime? You got yourself kidnapped and nearly murdered. You have absolutely no evidence whatsoever that those two men have been stealing. Just because you don't know why they're here and what they're doing, it doesn't make them criminals.'

'I shall get evidence. It can't be that hard. We can pop into the Unfurled Moth for a drink one evening and get into conversation with them, and if they're not there I can pretend to go to the toilet but instead go up and have a look around that Monty's room.'

'For goodness sake Celia! You can't go searching people's rooms, you're not Colombo. Why do you have this overwhelming need to make things right all the time, why can't you leave things alone?'

'I don't know Ronald, I expect it's the Virgo in me, I can't help it, I can't stand injustice, I've struggled with it all my life and I expect I always will. Look I'll be careful, I'll only ask a few questions here and there. Anyway, not to worry, I've got a feeling there's an angel watching over me,' Celia laughed, thinking of the collection of white feathers she had collected and hugged Ronald reassuringly.

What Sort of Club?

❦

Celia was feeling curious. She had received an email from Kevin Crossley who took the bookings for the parish hall.

To: Celia Ladygarden

From: Kevin Crossley

Re: Parish Hall

Hi Celia,

I've received the forwarded email, requesting to hire the hall on a regular basis from John Little.

Is that OK with you?

FORWARDED TO: Celia Ladygarden

From: John Little

To: Kevin Crossley

Re: Parish Hall

I would like to hire the hall every Tuesday morning

from 10.00 am to 12.00 am, for the next three months, starting September, October and November.

Would there be a discount for this block booking?

FROM: Kevin Crossley

To: Celia Ladygarden

What do you think Celia? I'm not sure we want to give him a discount.

To: Kevin Crossley

From: Celia Ladygarden

Re: John Little - CONFIDENTIAL

Kevin, I know you haven't lived here very long but you do know that everybody in the village calls him Blue John? He's captain of the cricket team and he's had many a maiden over behind the cricket pavilion, whilst his poor wife Eileen is rushed off her feet providing high quality teas.

My mother told me 'Never trust a hirsute man' and he has hair on every surface. We all know what sort of DVD collection he's got in his shed, pure SMUT! At least I know that all Ronald's got in his shed is a packet of digestives and the latest Lee Childs.

Have you met Valerie? He brought Valerie back from a business trip to Thailand. Apparently, he met her over cocktails in 'The Pink Lotus Pleasure House'. Poor Eileen is devastated but says at least she's good with the hoover.

Blue John insists she's a long-lost cousin but the only resemblance I can see is that they are both over six foot and sport a five o'clock shadow. She wears more makeup than Carol Vorderman and you wouldn't credit the size of her feet. She'll do alright in the Debenhams sales, there's always large sizes left. Anyway, I think we need to know EXACTLY what he and his 'friends' are going to get up to.

As to the block booking I don't think we can offer a discount. We don't give a discount to anyone else for block bookings and we don't want to start a precedent.

Perhaps you should remind him of the rules of hire of the hall. No offence but between you and me I don't trust the fellow.

Celia

FORWARDED to Celia Ladygarden
    To Kevin Crossley
    From John Little
    Hi Kevin, Yes I can quite understand re 'no discount', not a problem, we are happy to pay going rate. I'll collect key first Tuesday in September.
    Regards
    John

To: Kevin Crossley
    From Celia Ladygarden
    I note that John Little omitted to inform you as to

what purpose he wants to hire the hall. Knowing his proclivities, I think it's important that we know that before we hand over the key. Ask him? again!

Celia

FORWARDED to Celia Ladygarden

To: Kevin Crossley

From: John Little

Sorry Kevin, slipped my mind. We are starting a little club for a few friends. The only facilities we will use is the kettle to make tea and coffee.

Regards

John Little

To: Kevin Crossley:

From: Celia Ladygarden

Is it me or is John Little being evasive? We don't want a St Urith version of the Pink Lotus Pleasure House!

ASK HIM WHAT SORT OF CLUB!

Celia

FORWARDED to Celia Ladygarden

To: Kevin Crossley

From: John Little

Stamp collecting.

John

To: Kevin Crossley

From: Celia Ladygarden

Fair enough. It's good to have another club using the hall.

Don't say anything but I will pop in unannounced one Tuesday just to make sure it's philately and not fellatio because I have a funny feeling about this.

Max Cheetham

Max Cheetham was a handsome man somewhere in his early forties. He wore his light brown hair unfashionably long with silver threaded wings sweeping back from his lightly tanned face, Nigel Havers style. Always smartly dressed, his obviously tailor-made clothes fit well on his tall muscular frame. When Max had moved in there had been lots of speculation in St Urith about him.

Miss Worsnip told everyone who wouldn't listen that he was, 'one o'they smoothy types from Lunnun,who prey on wumun'.

Max was renting one of several cottages known as the 'Barracks' in a little hamlet a quarter of a mile out of the village but still in the parish. It is thought that Royalist troops were first housed there in the autumn of 1645 during the English civil war. Max had been told a little of this history by the letting agent and instead of keeping the low profile he had hoped for, he felt a bit like those besieged Royalist dragoons, as various villagers descended on him. Harold the cross-dressing librarian had popped around with a leaflet on the opening times of the mobile library and a couple of village ladies called on him with some cut-rounds and homemade jam, but to their annoyance none of them had been able to find out about his personal circumstances. Not one of them had made it over the threshold, as Max had literally blocked the door with his body. Celia Ladygarden was another kettle of fish entirely. Max had a feeling that she wouldn't give up so easily.

Max wore the illusion of a man of means with ease, although the truth was he lurched from one grand scheme to another, always living on the edge. This time was different, this time he knew he was onto a winner. He wasn't sure how but it seems he had signed himself up for the Parish Magazine and one of the first things he did after reading about it, was to make a generous donation to the Air Ambulance Landing Light Fund. Thus, having endeared himself to the locals in the village he hoped it would stop them prying into his business.

Max unlocked the back door of the house with the large brass key from the bunch he had collected off Sir Reginald that morning, and stepped into a hallway with what he thought would have been the boot room on one side and a utility room on the other. Entering the kitchen, he was struck by the magnificent fireplace on the opposite wall. It was a giant of a fireplace, carved in stone and with a raised flat hearth. Not entirely heartless, he was sorry as he realised that this was almost definitely going to be one of the items on his list. Whilst he had the house to himself he had a good look around. He was quite a romantic man and had enjoyed many a happy stay in the company of friends in some of the historical homes of England. He knew Stonepark was a Grade 11 listed building and he thought it beautiful. It wore its architectural features like a faded ball-gown and he wondered about the history it had seen in its lifetime. There was a bit of Max that was disturbed by the Russian's plans for the house, but not enough to turn down the lucrative contract that was going to fund his next visit to the hot-spots of the South of France.

Dipping into his dark blue leather man-bag he pulled out a sheaf of papers held together with treasury tags. As he walked into the middle of the kitchen he flipped through the pages until he found what he was looking for. 'Kitchen - 17c stone fireplace - Designation - Pool Room - Fitted as a seat'. Pulling off the duplicate sticker he stuck it on the fireplace. As he moved through the house checking off the various pieces, he thought about his client, a Russian Oligarch. Max hadn't actually met his client, but had been engaged by a third party on behalf of the Russian. The client had bought a property in Berkshire and it was to be completely refurbished. The Oligarch's nubile young wife had very definite ideas, given to her by a very expensive interior designer called Georges, about how she wanted it, and what she wanted she got. The

Oligarch had bought Stonepark house primarily for the stone fireplaces, pillars and statues, but it would also be useful as a further holiday home. He had employed Max to arrange and manage the removal and transportation of all the items his wife and the designer had chosen to be fitted into the new house in Berkshire.

It wasn't important or considered and obstacle that the property was Grade 11 listed and that it was against the law to remove anything of historic value. Max only hoped that they could get everything out without anyone noticing and reporting it. The Oligarch was keeping the property anyway, he was going to completely refurbish it and use it as a holiday home for family and friends, it wasn't likely that anyone local would get a look inside.

Max was amazed at the large sitting room with its huge windows and incredible uninterrupted views across to Dartmoor in the distance. The oldest fireplace was in this room, very early 17th Century, with decorated wood paneling. Max finished his inspection, sticking on the last of the labels from his lists. The next step would be to get Monty Butler and his team in to remove everything with a sticker on, pack it up, and let the Russian's men load it onto a lorry and transport it to Berkshire. The hardest part of this job would be carrying it out without anybody finding out until it was too late. And Max was finding out that keeping secrets in St Urith was not going to be easy, especially when there were busybodies like Celia on his case.

Celia Confides in Harold

❧

Celia hadn't seen Harold since she was in the library van a couple of weeks ago, so she was pleased to bump into him outside Betty's Buns and Batch. 'Hello Harold, did you get to the bottom of that piece of paper you showed me with the numbers and measurements on?' Celia asked.

'It did belong to that new Max chappie, but he didn't seem too pleased when I gave it back to him,' replied Harold.

'How so?' asked Celia.

'Well, he just grabbed it off me and said it wasn't important anyway and walked off. Proper rude, I thought,' complained Harold.

'Now you know it's not that I'm suspicious of the incomers in the village, we're not living in the dark ages, we welcome people in this village,' said Celia, 'but there's something not quite right about that Max Cheetham, I can feel it. Don't you think it's too much of a coincidence, that Max and Monty Butler arrived within a few days of each other? And they drink together in the Unfurled Moth.'

'You have got a suspicious nature Celia! But I must say I certainly noticed Monty when he arrived. I'm only sorry that he doesn't appear to be a reader as he hasn't made it into my library van yet,' Harold responded with a smile.

'I don't think you can assume he's not a reader Harold, most people read on devices these days. I do all my reading on my Kindle, even my library books. I do come to the library van to borrow knitting or sewing books though, so I still support you, don't I?' Celia asked.

'That's true. I know it's stupid, in this day and age, but I forget that some people prefer to read on their devices and never go near a library. I love the feel of a book and its new the smell, I'm just old-fashioned I guess. I shall have to hope that gorgeous man has a hobby and might want to borrow a reference book.'

'But that's my point, we don't know what he's into, hobbies or otherwise. He has a London accent but that doesn't mean much these days as people move around so much, he could come from anywhere.' Celia said.

'Max is posh, one of they public schoolboys I suspect,' Harold said.

'A minor public school I reckon, I suspect he's all talk and no trousers as my mother would have said.'

'I love your mum's sayings, she's sorely missed,' they both had a moment before Harold continued, 'but getting back to Max, he donated money to the Devon Air Ambulance landing light fund, so he must have a fair bit in the bank'.

'Not necessarily, it could be all show. Maybe he needs to make a good impression. Ruby thinks he's no good as well. I could be wrong, but I very rarely am, nor is Ruby,' Celia asserted, 'I think there is something going on in the village that shouldn't be going on, so keep your eyes and ears open Harold.'

'Ooh Celia, have you had one of your spooky feelings?' Harold asked.

Celia wondered whether she should mention the angels. Most people would think she was barking. Harold wouldn't though, and she'd helped him out a time or two before and knew she could trust him. A pure white feather floated down and landed on Harold's light brown hair. Celia looked at it in astonishment for a moment and tried to remember how many she had found now before reaching up and picking it off.

'I do have a strong feeling that something is going on Harold. There are a few woolly strands floating around in my head but at the moment I can't seem to knit them together. I think that Max Cheetham is one of those strands, and more than likely that chap Monty Butler, although he seems like a decent fellow. But can I ask you something Harold?' Celia hesitated before asking, 'have you seen any angels?'

Harold snorted with laughter, 'Angels! Celia, that's a bit fanciful even for you. The only angels I'm expecting to see are Angel cakes at my cake making class this evening with Dusty.'

'I'll thank you to have a little more respect Harold. I know it sounds fanciful but you know I wouldn't say anything unless I really believed it was true!' Celia said, hurt and a little tearful.

Harold's smile slid from his face as he realised how concerned and worried Celia really was and he immediately gave her a hug and apologised.

'Celia I'm really sorry, I should know better than to think you would say something without good reason. I can't say that I have seen any angels though and I think I might have noticed them. Although I am not really sure what you mean by Angels? I will keep my eyes and ears open and perhaps' (here a slow blush crept up his cheeks) 'I'll mention it to Inspector Pratt tonight.'

'Oh lord, no, please don't say anything to him, I'm not his favourite person. And if you start talking about Angels he will really think I'm a cream on top Cornish scone!'

'Heaven forbid!' laughed Harold.

Celia and Inspector Pratt have a symbiotic relationship, similar to the one the hippopotamus has with the little bird that cleans its teeth. The Inspector being the hippo dealing with the bigger things, and Celia the bird picking out the small bits that connect the bigger bits. They had come up against each other the year before when Celia had become unwittingly embroiled in three murders in their usually quiet little village.

'If you start mentioning me and angels in the same

sentence, you are likely to get it in the neck Harold. Better you don't say anything about me at all, just comment on the two men and what they might be up to in St Urith,' Celia protested.

Unfortunately, the thought of getting it, but preferably not in the neck as Celia was thinking, caused Harold to blush even more. He crouched down to hide it and stroked Hirsute Roley who immediately rolled over for a tummy rub, then with the other hand he stroked Polly who dropped down on her tummy, padded her front paws and pushed her hairy little face into Harold's knee.

'Dear little fur babies, they are so loving Celia, I'm really jealous. If ever the rules change and they allow dogs on the library bus, I'll be searching the dog rescue centres looking for my own little furbaby. Of course, if I was in a supporting loving relationship we could share the care and that would be better if we were to adopt a dog that had issues, like you did Celia,' Harold said, as a second blush crept up his neck to toast his cheeks.

'Ooh Harold, you're blushing, is there something I should know?' asked Celia.

'No!' answered Harold quickly but he kept his head down and fussed the dogs as he knew what Celia was like. She would keep on until she extracted the information by any means.

'How I wished I didn't tell-tale blush like a Pink-Faced Bald Uakari,' said Harold

'What the heck is a Pink-Faced whatsit? Anyway, stop trying to divert me. I think there is something going on,' Celia said in a singsong voice, 'now let me think, it must be something to do with your love life,' she smiled wickedly enjoying teasing Harold. 'The only new thing in your life is the baking lessons with Dusty Bins. Now I know that the object of your lust isn't going to be Dusty, because she is still going out with Billy Boy, even though he's away at Police College. Who else is taking the baking lessons Harold? For God's sake don't tell me it's Inspector Pratt!'

Poor Harold blushed again as he stood up protesting,'Celia, stop it, stop teasing, you know I've been on my own since Vincent went back to Brazil. Anyway, even if I was fond of some...'

Celia interrupted Harold before he could finish what he was saying.

'Harold! It is Inspector Pratt! Well, I didn't see that coming.' Celia was astounded, she would never have seen Harold and the Inspector as a couple.

'Celia, please, it's early days, we're just friends who enjoy baking together,' Harold protested.

'Baking, is that a euphemism Harold?'

'No, it isn't Celia, you have a mucky mind!' Harold admonished.

'Mmm sorry Harold, I shouldn't tease you, Inspector Pratt is lucky to have you as a friend. As he is a friend, perhaps you could mention that there might be something going on in the village that shouldn't be going on? But don't mention angels. Now I'd better be off, catch up with you again,' Celia gave Harold a quick hug before walking off with her dogs.

She hadn't got very far when Trixie Bell's young nephew came whizzing along on his scooter.

'Hello Chief, staying at your Auntie's, are you?' Celia asked.

Chief, using his foot as a brake, skidded to a stop. 'Yes, coz me mum's having a baby and I get to stay with auntie Trixie and eat buns from Bins.'

'That's nice, not too many buns I hope or you'll be sick,' Celia said with a smile.

'Sometimes I get to eat my food twice,' said Chief, whose father is a rugby fan and supports Exeter rugby team whose nickname is 'Exeter Chiefs'.

'Really? That's clever of you,' said Celia.

'I've got reflux,' said Chief.

'Oh, do you like having reflux?' asked Celia.

'Well, sometimes I get to eat my food twice,' Chief told her.

'Well, if it's something tasty that's lucky,' Celia said.

'Yea, it's great, bye,' Chief gave her a wave, did a fancy spin of his handlebars and sped off on his scooter.

The Hon Sharon Knowles

The Honourable Sharon Knowles, shiny conker brown tresses wild about her face, wiped up the last of her tomato sauce and egg with her bread soldier and popped it into her mouth as she rose from the kitchen table. Although she had cooked her breakfast herself it would be poor Mrs Budgen who would have to clear up the pots and the mess she had left behind. Mrs Budgen entered the kitchen just as Sharon was going out.

'Off to your 'orses little maid?' Mrs Budgen asked with a loving nudge of her hip as they passed in the doorway.

Sharon planted an eggy kiss on Mrs Budgen's cheek, 'Course Mrs B,' and went on her way. By 6.45 she was in the stables mucking out, feeding, watering and grooming her horses. Unfortunately for Mrs Budgen, who would have to wash at least seven pairs a week, Sharon was still wearing her pyjamas. Luckily for Sharon, Mrs Budgen would wash as many pairs of cast off pyjamas, and anything else, for her darlin' little maid. After showering and dressing in the en-suite she'd had built attached to the stables, Sharon went to the one and only male who had stolen her heart. Laying her head onto her horse's neck, her fingers gently working through his glossy coat, she murmured to him lovingly. Angelo was a fine Arabian, with the distinctive head shape and high tail carriage, born in 2009 of Sparkle Star. The horse pushed against her, then stamped a hoof, showing he was ready for a jaunt. Sharon led him out into the yard, his glossy chestnut coat shining in the early morning light. An energetic, strong natured horse, he lapped up the attention Sharon lavished on him. Bred for endurance, she would ride him for miles through the North Devon countryside and they both loved to jump. She saddled up, tightened the girth then hoisted herself up onto her soft calfskin leather saddle which allowed close contact with her horse.

The Hon Sharon was quite a sight as she trotted out of the yard and headed for the village. Not for her thick jodhpurs, shirt and hacking jacket, far too hot for a warm spring morning. The white floaty tunic, with Bluebell blue embroidered detail around the neck, was made of a fine soft and slightly transparent voile and had a slit up either side allowing her freedom of movement. Soft tan Ostrich style calfskin boots, handmade by Secchiari, encased her bare legs enhancing her naturally tanned thighs. The fabric of her tunic rose with the movement of her body, seeming to hover in the air before settling around her voluptuous curves. A wreath of white daisies was entwined in her hair and a pair of blue Gucci sunglasses adorned her face.

As she trotted along, she thought about her mother, what a surprise that had been. She was certainly following in her mother's footsteps, chuckled Sharon to herself. Although she would miss her, she understood her mother's reasons for going, in fact she rather admired her. There was no chance of her visiting her in Africa, she couldn't leave her precious horses, but perhaps they could video-call. Sharon didn't know how on earth her father was going to cope without his Lady Marigold but it was his own fault. Over the years he had stopped doing anything to help with the estate and house. Not interested in anything other than racing, he'd spent more and more time at the track. Sharon didn't know why her mother had put up with it for so long. She felt guilty herself because she too had relied on her mother for so many of those same boring tasks that her father had. As she trotted on, she wondered how her father was going to handle the news when he found out. She'd seen the large brown envelope that arrived with hers that morning. It had her father's name on it, in her mother's writing and she guessed at its contents.

In some ways the loss of Stonepark, her grandparent's house, had hurt her more than her mother's defection. So much of her life had been spent there with her grandparents and their dogs. When her grandfather died, Gip the Jack Russell had pined away and died three weeks later of a broken heart. Red, the liver and white Springer Spaniel, had clung to her grandmother after losing her furry companion but had taken to life in France being the only, spoilt, dog. It was her grandmother a passionate horsewoman herself who had taught her to ride, sitting her on her first Dartmoor pony when she was about two. Grandmother and only granddaughter had a special bond, and although Sharon was pleased she was living happily in France, she still missed her. Still, France was doable, she could easily take her horses over for an extended visit.

Not surprisingly that morning in St Urith there was a sprinkling of the male population who had managed to find some reason to be in the main street of the village on this sunny day, hoping to catch an eyeful of the Hon Sharon. This particular morning Monty Butler, wearing just a pair of white linen shorts, his muscular thighs astride the first-floor window sill of his room in The Unfurled Moth, was leaning out rolling a cigarette. Not that he was interested in the Hon Sharon, there was only one woman for Monty, and she had captured his heart forever. No, he was just having a smoke out of the window because smoking was banned in his rented room.

The landlord Fred Dimmock had strolled out of the

front door, drying a beer mug with a tea-towel that was held together by stains. He was aware of cigarette smoke floating down from his first-floor room but didn't acknowledge it. He had no intention of killing the golden goose - Monty's rent money was his lifeline.

Willie was making his egg delivery rounds on his rickety old bicycle with the wooden egg crates tied on with baler twine, front and back. Stopping outside of the Unfurled Moth, he balanced himself on his bicycle by holding himself up on his one and only arm. Unfortunately, his grubby hand, which had only recently been thrust underneath some startled chickens, rested on the gleaming paintwork of Max Cheatham's shiny silver Jaguar. It was a 1963 E type, the love of his life and the only real possession that Max owned. Max, who had parked outside the Unfurled Moth in the hope of having a quick word with Monty, was horrified at this assault. He jumped out, polishing cloth in hand and tried to protect his precious car by squeezing himself in between the car and Willie's bicycle, whilst at the same time keeping his nose as far away from Willie's roaming aroma as possible.

'Here steady old chap,' admonished Max to Willie.

'That's wot I be doin,' replied Willie, unpeeling his sticky hand from the Jag, wobbling a bit and slapping his hand back down, as if to demonstrate.

It wasn't the smell of Willie's chickens that was offensive, he looked after them very well. They had a cosy barn and access into the fresh air, and if you were to pick one up and have a sniff they mostly smelled of cotton. No, it was Willie's own personal aroma that was to be avoided, as Max was finding out. And his filthy stories. In fact, unless you wanted fresh eggs, Willie was to be avoided at all costs.

As the Hon Sharon slowly made her way down into the village from Copshott Hall, there was an added bonus for the watchers as the morning's sunshine illuminated Sharon's body through the diaphanous material of her tunic. Tommy Alcock and Eric Beech, neighbours and snooker rivals, were working on their vegetable patches in the front gardens of their adjoining cottages which were opposite the Unfurled Moth. Tommy paused in the act of digging a trench, leant on his garden spade, and nodded casually to Eric over the fence, 'a light shower would be welcome.'

Eric, who was hoeing his beets, also stopped and, leaning on his hoe, replied 'ground's dry.'

The Hon Sharon seemed oblivious to the salacious looks from the men and the tuts of disapproval from Miss Worsnip, who was stood in the doorway about to enter Betty's Buns & Batch.

'Shame on you! You should be ashamed of yourselves, grown men leering at a young girl like that!' Miss Worsnip berated the men. It's 2018 for goodness sake!

'Quite right Miss Worsnip, you tell em, now what can I get you?' asked Betty from behind her counter.

Sharon was most surprised to hear Miss Worsnip defend her and called out to her, 'morning Miss Worsnip.'

As she drew nearer to the Unfurled Moth, Cat drove up in her jaunty yellow van and slowed, stopping to chat with Sharon astride her horse. This effectively shielded Sharon from all the men except for Tommy and Eric, who, having exhausted the subject of the weather were now talking snooker and had forgotten the girl completely. Cat and Sharon chatted through the open passenger window. They had become friends after meeting when Cat had called at Copshott Hall to wash, cut and set Mrs Budgen's hair, after being recommended by Ruby Bins. Sharon was pleased to see Cat as, contrary to what her mother might think, she was missing her and feeling a bit lonely. She had yet to discover that her mother had no intention of returning to Devon, as she had left the house early for the stables, long before her father had even risen from the comfort of his bed, let alone read his post. The two young women agreed to meet up later. Cat would drive over to Sharons and they planned to watch a film, drink wine and eat popcorn, and Cat was going to sleep over.

Fred, landlord of The Unfurled Moth was denied his lusting of the Hon Sharon by the position of Cat's bright yellow van. Thwarted, he looked around for another target of his attention and saw Harold, the cross-dressing librarian. Fred seized any opportunity to taunt Harold so called out, 'Er dresses better 'an you yung Arold.'

Harold stopped. A well brought up young man, taught to turn away meanness with kindness, he looked

Fred in the eye and said, 'I've ordered a book for you Fred, it will be in the mobile Library on Tuesday.'

'I bain't ordered no book, what you'm on about,' Fred replied, forgetting his nasty gibe.

Although well brought up and kind, Harold wasn't averse to a little teasing of his own, 'I heard you were struggling to keep the pub going and was looking to start a second business. This book is all about starting up your own holiday park,' Harold smiled, then walked swiftly on and turned into Betty's Bins Buns & Batch.

Fred, steam coming out of his ears yelled, 'Willie you'm little bugger come 'ere, it twere sposed to be a secrit!'

Before Fred could even move Willie had jumped on his bike and wheels wobbling, eggs jiggling made for the drang leading to his place. Fred, knowing it was a waste of time going after Willie, turned, grumbling to himself and shuffled back into his pub.

Monty, who had watched the goings on from his seat in the upstairs window, was thinking about Stonepark. He'd found out a little bit about the history of it. It was a fine example of a small Devon Manor and although it was empty, clearly had been a family home. The plaster work was impressive with plaster friezes around the walls and some central decorative motifs. One bedroom had a magnificent barrelled ceiling with decorative plasterwork and the fireplace in this room was of carved oak with inset tessellated tiles. There were a few of these oak fire surrounds and luckily the oligarch had not wanted these removed. Monty couldn't help feeling sorry for Fred. He'd found him a grumpy old man but having found out some of the reason why, felt sorry for him. He knew that Fred was struggling both financially and with the physical effort needed to run the pub single-handedly. He did what he could to help in little ways but Fred wasn't the easiest of men to help. Monty stubbed his cigarette out and popped the butt into a small tin he kept on the windowsill, then locking the door behind him went down into the saloon and leant on the bar.

'Is Harold right Fred, are you thinking of starting another business?'

'Bain't nobody's bizness but mine,' muttered Fred. He liked Monty but he wasn't going to share his personal business.

'Quite right Fred, but as you know I run my own business, same as you, and I reckon us entrepreneurs should stick together and help each other out.'

'Ere bain't you go using thikky words!' Fred scowled and moved down the bar to polish his pumps with a grubby rag.

'Erm right, er well, all I meant was we're both men of business.' Monty smiled winningly at Fred, who missed it as he hadn't raised his head.

'Right well, it's jest an idea an me an Willie don't want none pinching it.'

'Quite right and me lips are sealed mate,' Monty replied.

Fred liked Monty and he needed him to stay at the pub. He didn't want him renting anywhere else as the rent from his room was the only money that was keeping him afloat. Apart from that he was still unsure about his and Willie's idea.Perhaps, he thought, Monty would be the ideal person to run it pass.

'Well I got some o'they bell tents from a fella I knowd and that bit o'land back o'my place could be one o'they glamping places. Willie's place backs on t'mine and ee's gonna ave ees ens fer a pettin.'

'Sorry mate you lost me at 'ens fer a pettin,' Monty responded.

'Ens! Willie's ens, the kiddies can stroke em and pettum,' Fred explained.

'Oh right, hens, I get it. Ere Fred, I think it's a cracking idea, get it Fred? Cracking?' Monty chuckled.

Fred, who had moved up the bar closer to Monty and bent over the bar conspiratorially when he was telling him about his idea, now stood up as straight as his bent back allowed.

'Oh yer think tiz funny do yer? Think I bain't clever enough to run one o'thay oliday places?'

Monty rushed to assure Fred, 'No, no, Fred I wasn't laughing at you or your idea, I think it's brilliant. I was just making a silly joke, you know. Look, Willie, eggs, cracking idea, cracking eggs?'

Fred gave Monty a pitying look, 'Vool! I tell 'ee my boody, uz's gotta do zummat to keep the ole Muff. Uz Dimmock's ave ad an and in thikky Muff fer genera-tions, uz bain't be the one 'ooze gonna lose er.' Fred wiped his leaky eyes with the dirty rag.

Monty sympathised with Fred who was quite

clearly upset, but he struggled to contain his laughter at the thought of each generation of the Dimmock's with a hand in the Muff. It had taken him awhile to get used to Fred and Willie calling 'The Unfurled Moth', The Unkept Muff, but this was something else.

Willie sidled into the bar 'I tell 'ee, mister 'ee be proper cradded smornin. Come on me boody, 'tiz time t' wet me oozle.'

'Yer gurt dawbake! Gurt guzzle guts be good fer nort, ee's es much good es a dug with zide pockets,' Fred said to Willie as he slammed down on the bar a pint of Scrumpy Cider.

Monty observed the two men with increasing puzzlement. He hadn't a clue as to what they were talking about as Fred's accent became stronger when talking to Willie and Willie's was nearly unintelligible anyway, but as there didn't appear to be any animosity between them he presumed that whatever was said wasn't contentious. He wasn't so sure about Willie's cider though. Dark browny orange in colour, it looked as if it was going to climb out of the glass and slap Willie about the face! Willie, in a matey way, shoved his armless shoulder into Monty who wasn't expecting it. Unfortunately for Willie, Monty was built like a Devon privy and Willie bounced off and spun around the other way. He stood there for a while looking blankly at the door wondering where his Scrumpy had gone before turning back, picking his tankard up and taking an enormous swig. Willie turned to Monty and said,

'You'm wanna cut off thikky ade of an eel an rub thikky bloody ade over that wart. Then, bury ees' ade, an' as ee' rots away, so twill wart.'*

Monty who hadn't understood a word of what Willie was saying to him, picked up the metal tankard Fred had put in front of him anticipating the malty slightly sweet taste of the pale hoppy ale offered by the Exmoor Gold. Chinking the tankard against Willie's he toasted, 'and cheers to you too,' before taking a great swallow. Immediately his eyes started watering, his face screwed up and he started coughing. Fred and Willie both chuckled at the sight of Monty bent over supporting himself by both hands on the bar. Fred went to top up Monty's tankard from an old military jerry can, 'second mouthfuls best, sup up.'

Willie chuckled, 'Yer be nort but 'n ole guzzle guts.'

Monty managed to splutter, 'No way Jose, you can drink that Cider Willie, I'll have half a pint of Exmoor Gold thanks Fred, in a glass, so I can see what I'm drinking, I've got to drive later!'

'Ther's a lot a Cocks in St Urith,' Willie said to no one in particular, but as there was only Monty and Fred in the pub, Monty assumed it was to him.

'Specially in the graveyard. I'm a Cock, spect that's why I keeps ens.' Unfortunately, Willie had just taken a mouthful of scrumpy and as he always laughed at his own jokes, he coughed spluttered and a fair bit of Scrumpy came out of his nose. Willie picked the bar towel up, wiped his nose then mopped up the coughed up splattered cider and then spread the towel back down on the bar.

Monty didn't fancy his beer anymore and with a 'cheers', went up to his room to change his T-shirt which had benefited from a Willie splashing.

The Desecration of Stonepark

M onty's team of three men and one woman had nearly finished removing all the architectural features at Stonepark that were listed on the schedule they had been working from. There were classical Bath stone masks of men and lions, gate posts, and intricately carved stone Corinthian capitals that had been chosen as legs for a dining table. A cast iron mask of Poiseidon and a large 17th Century fireplace on a raised hearth to be used as seating were both destined for the pool room. A carved stone armorial panel and a second 17th Century carved stone fireplace, plus a few statues and other bits and pieces. They had all been wrapped in protective bubble wrap and cardboard and were resting on pallets, waiting to be loaded up and taken away. The only piece left was the large fireplace in the kitchen and they were waiting for Monty to come and help them with it. Once that one was off the wall and all packed up they could take their money and head back to London. The three men and one woman had paid for their stay and packed up the caravan back in Umberleigh they had been staying in and it was ready to be hitched onto the back of their van for a quick getaway. Now they were stood leaning on the van waiting for Monty to arrive and help them with the large fireplace and to pay them off before they headed back to London.

Monty arrived at last and they all went into the house. He and his workforce were stood looking at the fireplace when they heard a vehicle pull up outside, then footsteps coming towards them.

'Flippin Nora!' Em shrieked at the sight of the two men that barrelled through the door.

Monty's phone went off at the same time, it was Max calling.

'Monty, two of the Oligarch's men will be arriving sometime today and they will be removing the last fireplace and they will also fit the replacement. Now don't argue, he's paying and it will save your guys from having to do it. You'll still get paid the same. Now get yourselves out of there and leave it to his men, I'll see you in the pub later.'

'Right you lot we're finished here, c'mon, Monty said.

'But Monty...' Em started to speak, but Monty interrupted her,

'I said we're finished here, c'mon, out everyone,' Monty ordered them, and headed for the door which was blocked by two solid Russian bodies.

'OK fellers, it's all yours,' Monty said as he smiled at the men.

They stood for a moment longer arms folded, staring, and then moved silently aside allowing Monty and his troop to leave. Once outside, he paid off his team and they climbed into their van and drove off to collect their caravan and then back to London. Monty drove back to St Urith and the Unfurled Moth glad to be finished with the job. He was glad that they hadn't had to remove the last fireplace. It was magnificent and looked so right where it was. He'd felt deeply unhappy about ripping out fireplaces and all the other statues and fittings at Stonepark. An experienced salvager with many years of experience, Monty had great respect for buildings and it went against his principles to destroy what was undoubtedly a listed building, even though Max had assured him that it wasn't. He wasn't sure what to do. He'd paid his guys off and they would be safe out of it back in London but Monty had a dilemma. If he took the money for the job, he and Max would be gone from St Urith and it was unlikely that anybody would find out about the destruction in the house as the Oligarch was putting in replacement fireplaces and keeping it, so it wouldn't be going back on the market. But if he left St Urith it was unlikely that he would ever see Lilac Davenport again, and he was not sure that he could bear that.

Allcock & Daisy

Tommy Alcock stopped at the church and pinned up the list for the following Saturday's bell-ringing tour. He knew if he didn't do it now on his way back from Betty's Buns and Batch he would forget it later. Daisy, his small tan and white Jack Russell, waited patiently as he locked up the arched oak door in the bell tower. They followed their usual evening route with Daisy trotting on ahead sniffing her way along the lane. Tommy, munching his bun, could hear noise coming from further on and presumed it was either the new people at last moving in to Stonepark, the house that lay further along the lane, or the workmen that had been working there for the past few months. Although nobody had actually seen the workmen, Tommy's aunt Olive's neighbour June's daughter cleaned the farm-house at the caravan site where they were staying. June's daughter had been rather taken with Tony, one of the workmen, and would find excuses to bump into him, even arriving very early for work in the hopes of catching him before he left the site. This had given the owners of the park quite a shock as June's daughter hadn't once been on time for work in the six months she had worked there, let alone arrive early.

Tony was a good-looking chap and knew it, he enjoyed a bit of flirtation and the flattering attention of June's daughter but he had a beautiful wife and children back in London and June's daughter was going to be disappointed. Early one morning, June's daughter had waylaid him on his way back from the shower block and not wanting to upset the girl, he had stopped and chatted. The others were ready to go and were getting in the van when Em called out to Tony.

'Tone! Get a move on you lazy git, Stonepark won't wait you know,' her and Charlie smirked as he jumped in the van, neither of them realised that Em had given the house name away.

It didn't take long before everybody in St Urith knew they were working there, but nobody had been able to get any information out of them, as to what work they were doing. Tommy thought this was the ideal opportunity to find out what work the new owners were having done before they moved in. Wouldn't hurt to take a look and see what was going on, he thought, might even keep him ahead of the gossips for once. The gate was open so he wandered down the drive, Daisy by his side. As he neared the front door he saw a lorry with its back open, parked outside the open front door. Curious to see what was going on and as there wasn't anybody about, he walked towards the back of the lorry just as the back of Max Cheetham appeared through the door, followed by two burly men carrying something that looked rather heavy.

Tommy backed away as all hell kicked off. Daisy started barking, the two burly men started shouting in some foreign language that he had never heard before and Max, after stopping and standing with his mouth open for a couple of seconds, joined in with the shouting but added in gesticulating arms! Walking briskly away, Daisy still growling, Tommy had just made it to the end of the drive when Max caught up with him.

'Hold on fella,' Max said, taking Tommy's arm in a tight grip, turning him so his back was to the house and bringing him to a stop.

Daisy was not happy at her master being manhandled and started snarling and barking madly whilst running around and around the two men who had to shout to make themselves heard over her noise.

'Does she bite?' Max asked nervously as he hitched his leg up each time Daisy got near.

'Yes! 'specially when someone is attacking her dad. Now let me go!'

'Dad?' quite clearly the man was mad thought Max, 'sorry old chap, no harm done eh?' Max wheedled as he tried to smooth down Tommy's jacket sleeve, which was pointless as the creases and wrinkles were a permanent part of Tommy's 'look' and had been there longer than Daisy had.

'What's going on anyway? What's with all the shouting? And they furriners?'

Tommy had a strong local accent, but Max had learnt to tune his ear during his stay in the village and managed to pick out most of it.

'There's nothing going on, the new owners are private people that's all, you can understand that I'm sure, Eric is it?'

Tommy, not stupid, decided not to correct Max about his name, but keen to get away responded with 'daft buggers!' and whistled to Daisy who was now barking furiously before shrugging off Max and heading out of the drive.

Tommy didn't make it. The two Russians had come up behind him, having walked silently on the grass instead of the noisy gravel. One of the men threw a rope over his head and tightened it around his waist trapping his arms, the second man threw a sack over daisy and scooped her up tying it tight at the top.

'Don't you hurt my dog, I'm warning you, don't you dare hurt her,' Tommy yelled at the man whilst struggling to free himself.

'Gentlemen, there is no need for this, I'm dealing with the situation, Eric is on his way home, there is no problem,' Max protested.

'There's a problem now yerz, pair of idiots, yerz proper mazed, I'm gonna report you!'shouted Tommy.

'No need for that, Eric, there has been a mistake that's all,' Max put a hand on one of the Russians arms, whose width was about the size of Max's waist. 'Look chaps, no need for this, let Eric go on his way, no hassle, what do you say?'

'We say, Max, go home, leave us to deal with this little problem,' one of the Russians said as the two muscle men pushed Tommy back down the drive towards the house.

'I'm not a little problem, I'll be a big problem for you two if you don't let me go, this is sleepy St Urith not an England versus Russia football match!' shouted Tommy.

The talking Russian, as opposed to the one that just grunted, tightened the rope around Tommy and whispered in his ear. If there was a competition between Tommy and Max as to who could look the palest it would be a close-run thing but Tommy would just pip the post as the blood drained from his face. Max, choosing discretion over valour got in his car. The sooner I'm finished with this job and out of here the better he thought, and drove away without looking back.

Celia Takes a risk

❧

Celia had kept up a long vigil at her sitting room window with the binoculars, watching for Max's car to come down the hill. There was only a little stretch of the road that you could actually see the cars, which was right at the top, hence the binoculars. After that, the high Devon banks with their thick hedges hid any vehicles from view. Of course, Ronald kept asking her what she was looking for and although initially satisfied with her response of rabbits, then birds, was, after fifty-four minutes, suspicious.

'What, or who are you looking for?' he asked, 'You're up to something again, aren't you?'

'For goodness sake Ronald, I'm just looking out of the window at the fields and animals, that's all.'

'Pull the other one. I know you too well Celia and you are definitely watching for someone.'

'Huh, you can talk Ronald. Who is it who keeps an

eye on the comings and goings up our road? Not me but you.'

'That's different,' replied Ronald

'Hmm... well you'll be happy now because I'm going to take Polly out for a walk, 'Celia said as she put down the binoculars and went to fetch Polly's harness and lead.

'I'm not taking Roley because I'm going for a longer walk and it will be too much for him,' Celia told Ronald as she struggled to put the bright pink harness on the bouncy Shih Tzu.

The real reason was Hirsute Roley, being a terrier, might well bark at anything, whereas Polly was the quietest dog, unless of course she heard someone coming or someone came to the door. In this instance, that warning was just what Celia needed but she hoped that wasn't going to happen. Calling out 'bye' to Ronald, she set off down the road. At the bottom, she turned right and headed up the lane. It was a lovely day for a walk and normally she would have asked her dear friend Gloria who lived down the road to come with her, but not today. So busy thinking and concentrating on getting to the top as soon as possible, she barely noticed the banks with an array of wild flowers and ferns. Celia was puffing as she reached the top of the hill out of the village. It was quite a climb. Not that it seemed to bother Polly who was as bouncy as ever and had thought the walk too slow.

Turning left at the top, Celia made her way to The

Barracks,* and making sure there was nobody about, made her way around to the back of the cottages. Having arrived at the back door of the one she was interested in, she realised that she hadn't quite thought things through. She had no idea how was she going to be able to get inside without a key. She peered through the small kitchen window, then tried to push up the sash but it was locked from the inside. Just as well really. she thought, I'm not really built for climbing in small windows. Polly, who obviously thought she was going to have a lovely visit and that there might be biscuits on offer, stood up on her back legs and started scratching vigorously at the door which slowly creaked open. Well it's not as if I'm breaking in, thought Celia, and before she could think about the consequences of being caught, she quickly stepped inside the kitchen and pulled the door to, but not shut behind her.

She stood for a moment listening for any sound, but the cottage felt empty. She relaxed and tried to get a feel for the place. She hadn't been in one of these cottages for some years, this one had been regularly rented out as a holiday cottage until Max Cheetham had moved in. She presumed he had a special arrangement. Well, he hasn't exactly moved in thought Celia, as she made her way into the sitting room and found it looking exactly like a holiday cottage without a personal object in sight. Better check though she thought, I only need to find one piece of evidence linking them to these robberies and I can go to the police with my suspicions. She unclicked Polly from her lead and lett her wander around. Unfortunately, the first thing Polly did was wander over to the rug in front of the wood burner, squat and do a wee.

'Oh, for goodness sake Polly! Why on earth did you do that? Oh well, he probably won't notice, will he?' she looked down at the spreading stain, 'well let's hope not.'

Celia opened each of the two drawers in the small oak dresser but all they revealed were a few brochures for local attractions, a guest book for people to write their reviews, and an information folder about the cottage. 'Come on Polly, let's have a look upstairs.' Celia made her way up the narrow staircase and stood still at the top of the landing. There was a small bathroom and a second door into a tiny bedroom that didn't look as if it had been used at all, but Celia checked the chest of drawers just in case.

She paused outside of the second bedroom. Could she really search through the bedroom of a man she didn't know? She didn't even rummage through Ronald's bits! What on earth am I doing? I need to get out of here. She turned and called to Polly who had jumped up on the bed in the little bedroom. 'Come on Polly let's get out of here,' Celia looked at Polly who stayed where she was but put her little head on one side and giving Celia a quizzical look through her big brown eyes. 'What? You think we've come this far, it would be silly not to check this last room? You're right sweetie.' Celia opened the door and her first impression of the room was surprise at how tidy it was, although it did feel as if it was used unlike the other rooms. There wasn't an item of clothing anywhere, not so much as a used tissue, let alone stolen goods but this was the only place left in the cottage where they could be hidden. The double bed was made neatly in military style and when Celia opened the wardrobe everything was hung immaculately, not a bent shirt cuff in sight. The shirts were colour coordinated, whites then blues, and some still had the dry- cleaning plastic over them. There were a couple of pairs of linen trousers followed by two linen jackets and a grey striped suit. The shoes were lined up in pairs on the bottom of the wardrobe.

The oak wardrobe was one of those old- fashioned sorts with a narrow door opening and a mirror on the back of the door. Celia reached around the opening into the space to the left of the door and Bingo! She put her hands on an old-fashioned attaché case. Putting it down on the bed, she hoped that it wasn't locked. It was a beautiful thing, a light buttery brown leather and probably made in the 1940's thought Celia. It was a similar style to a lawyer's case with two straps either side of the front and a locking clasp in the center. The straps weren't fastened and when she clicked the lock it popped open. What luck, she thought. Inside were various bundles of papers, one wad was held together by treasury tags. She was very carefully pulling it out when Polly started a low growling.

'Polly? Here sweetie, come to mummy,' Celia called

quietly and scrabbled in her pocket for a treat at the same time as pulling out the papers. She just had time to see the name Stonepark at the top of the first page before thrusting them back inside. Scooping up Polly, who had come at her call, she popped a treat in her mouth, shut the attaché case up and pushed it back inside the wardrobe, then tiptoed out of the room. Polly's hearing was exceptional considering how much hair she had so Celia was hoping that she still had time to get out of the cottage before whoever it was arrived. She had reached the bottom of the stairs when she heard someone at the front door which opened directly into the sitting room. Could she make it from there to the back door before Max opened it and saw her? If caught there was nothing she could say in her defense, he would have every right to call the police. With her hand around the mouth of Polly who was still managing a low growl at the back of her throat, Celia moved swiftly to the back door and stepped out, not stopping to put Polly down until she was back around and in front of the cottages. Putting Polly down Celia pulled a brown felt beret out of her pocket, rammed it on her head and started walking as fast as she could without breaking into a run, little Polly's legs going to and fro like pistons on a steam train.

Once she had put a fair distance between The Barracks and herself, she slowed down and then stopped, letting Polly have a sniff at an interesting clump of weeds. Celia looked down on the village of St Urith below her and let the peace of the beautiful countryside settle and quiet her mind. The fields of green went on as far as the eye could see. They surrounded the compact village with the church tower in the center, dominating the scene, and the rest of the buildings set all around as if to protect it. She carried on walking down the lane towards the village and opened her mind to what she had seen, wondering what Max and Monty might be up to in relation to Stonepark. Admitting she was wrong was not something Celia enjoyed, but she had to admit that she had been wrong about Max Cheetham and his friend Monty. They weren't the people who had been stealing from the National Trust properties. The fact that there wasn't any sign of stolen goods in Max's cottage wasn't in itself proof, but when Celia was in the cottage she had felt that her theory was completely wrong. Max was obviously a very organised man, he was well spoken and probably public school educated thought Celia. Whatever he was up to she guessed from what she had glimpsed on the papers that it had to do with Stonepark. All she had managed to see apart from the name was what looked like a list and possibly some measurements.

Harold had told her that it had been Max who had borrowed the book about local houses from the library, and there had been a list of measurements tucked inside it. Could that be something to do with Stonepark? Of course, it could well be completely legitimate, Stonepark had been sold so she had heard, so it was quite likely that the new owners were having some work done. But Max was definitely secretive about what he was doing and she didn't believe that he was writing a book, that didn't wash at all. Celia was an avid note booker and was always buying them and would always have one about her person with a pencil and a pen. Whenever she had an idea or heard an amusing conversation she would jot it down. There was no order to these jottings, it was just important to her to write them down. She would refer to them when she came to write the pantomime and they were rich with ideas and jokes. If Max really was a writer, even if he didn't write in notebooks, presumably there would be a laptop or a folder or some evidence of his writing in the cottage he had rented to write his book in. Of course, he could have his laptop with him and she knew she was old fashioned in writing in notebooks and a lot of writers kept everything on their devices, but somehow, she didn't believe he was writing a book. If Max was involved in some work that was going on at Stonepark, why not say? Why was it so secretive? And if Max was involved, then surely Monty must be as well, which, for a reason that Celia didn't want to acknowledge, made her sad. She was quite taken with Monty.

As she walked up her road and saw Ronald hovering anxiously in the window, she thought poor Ronald, he's right, I shouldn't get involved in whatever is going on. I can't quite believe what I've just done, searching someone's house, what was I thinking? What If I'd got caught? What would Ronald say? It's ridiculous. it's not as if anybody has been hurt or there has been a murder like last time. I'm going to stop thinking about Max and Monty. Well, I might think about Monty, I'm thinking he could feature in many a fantasy, thought Celia with a smile as she let herself into her home.

Stamp Collecting

Celia had agreed to meet Aunty Pat at the Parish
Hall as Aunty Pat was bringing some costumes
for the village panto that her cousin who lived down in
Lostwithiel had donated as being surplus to require-
ments at her local WI. Once they had put the costumes
away in the storeroom, they were going around to
Celia's as Aunty Pat had decided she wanted purple
streaks in her badly dyed fiery orange hair, and if you
are eight three, thought Celia, you can have whatever
hair colour you want and had agreed to do it for her.
Aunty Pat was already waiting at the Parish Hall when
Celia arrived with her key. She was wearing a tiger
print cotton catsuit with the legs cut off, and a pair of
her favourite jelly shoes (she seemed to have them in
every colour) with matching tiger print nail and toe
varnish. Her hair was in two high pigtails with purple
furry pom-poms on the ends and she was leaning on
her bonnet looking out over the playing fields.

'God's own country, Debn,' she greeted Celia with.

There were several cars parked outside the Parish Hall and when Celia looked the curtains were closed. Hmm... why would they need to close the curtains for a stamp collecting club? she thought. It was opportune that Aunty Pat was bringing the costumes in to the Parish Hall, it gave Celia an opportunity to see what John Little was up to.

'Leave the costumes in your car for a moment Aunty Pat, I want to see what's going on in here. Ssh, quiet now,' Celia slid the key in the lock and carefully opened the hall door.

They tiptoed through the vestibule, then Aunty Pat positioned herself behind one of the double doors leading into the main hall and Celia stood behind the other. There was thumping and shouts coming from inside.

'One, two, three, push,' said Celia and they pushed both doors open.

What a sight met their eyes. Neither Celia nor Aunty Pat said a word for about three seconds, then Aunty Pat started laughing and Celia couldn't help but join in. The members of the club hadn't even noticed the two women arrive and were enthusiastically carrying on with their activity, and it didn't involve stamps. A vigorous game of table tennis was in progress while the other members of the club were sat around on the hall chairs cheering the players on. It was a mixed doubles match. John Little was partnering a woman Celia didn't know against the funny little lay-preacher who always became so excited with religious fervour when he was giving a reading, that he would bounce up and down on his tippy toes and jiggle one hand in his pockets as if he was doing something he shouldn't be. Oh, how happy Celia was to see who his doubles partner was. Angela, fishing, Baker. The two women had crossed swords quite a few times since Angela had moved into St Urith. The woman was an absolute pain in Celia's eyes, and she wasn't that popular with many others. She thought she was a cut above everybody else in the village and had tried to get herself on various committees. The ones she had managed to bulldoze her way onto she had tried to boss everyone around and change things. Celia was pretty easy going and liked most people, but the worst thing that Angela fishing Baker had done was attack one of her most loved and special occupations. She had protested against the village pantomime.

Now, Celia was always very open to suggestions from the cast regarding the panto. It was very much a collaboration. She may have written the script but the players brought so much else to the story and would come up with funny ideas and jokes. Angela fishing Baker had weaseled herself onto the Parish Hall committee and under the guise of 'Any Other Business' demanded that the committee review the script of the next pantomime to ensure that there were no 'smutty jokes', no 'sexual innuendo' or 'skimpy outfits'. And if they did find any, then the script would have to be changed or the panto cancelled, otherwise it could bring disrepute on the Parish Hall Committee. There had been gasps of indrawn breaths and some of the committee members slid their chairs backwards out of the line of fire. Celia had soon put her in her place.

'Disrepute! Have you ever seen a pantomime Angela? That's what they consist of, sexual innuendos and silly jokes, and as for the skimpy costumes, it's usually only the men who wear them and certainly no children. If you cut all those things out, there would be no panto left! For your information, I would never write anything distasteful or inappropriate and most of the innuendos go over the young children's heads. We have been performing these pantomimes successfully for nineteen years and I have forty-six years of experience in the theatre. How many years' experience have you got Angela! fishing! Baker!?'

Before this could escalate any further, Gloria stepped in, much to everyone else's relief.

'I just wanted to say that the fundraising is going very well for the lighting for the air ambulance. The Parish Council have offered a large donation so that will mean the Air Ambulance can go ahead with installing the lighting.'

The meeting was wound up with haste amongst a cacophony of noise as chairs were scraped back, papers gathered up and everybody started leaving, chattering excitedly. Tommy Alcock and Eric Beech were chatting as they left the hall.

'Did Celia really call her Angela, fishing, Baker?' Tommy asked.

'I do believe she did,' replied Eric.

'You know what Celia means when she uses the word fishing,' stated Tommy.

'I do believe I do,' replied Eric

'Well it could have been worse,' said Tommy.

'It could with Celia,' confirmed Eric.

Angela fishing Baker had also caused ructions when she reported Fred at the Unfurled Moth to the Health and Safety department at the council and then put in a complaint to the planning department about the Speedwells because she didn't think it was quite the thing to have an undertaker in the village. Oh yes, Celia was going to enjoy this. She was about to make her presence known when Angela, saggy breasts flying, enthusiastically leaped for a shot and whacked the ping pong ball so hard it bounced off the table and rolled down the hall and stopped in front of Auntie Pat's feet. A great whoop had gone up at the shot and then deathly silence when Celia and Auntie Pat were noticed. There was a flurry of activity as several sets of hands tried to cover up their important naked parts.

Celia was always surprised that naturists were happy to carry out every possible activity without a qualm, including, obviously, naked table tennis, but the minute fully clothed people appeared they become self-conscious.

'I've never seen so many wrinkly bits in one place, pity we haven't got an iron,' chortled Aunty Pat.

Yes, John Littles stamp collecting club was in fact a naked table tennis club.

'Good morning all, would it be OK if we put some costumes in the store room please? It won't take more than five minutes?' Celia gaily called out.

John Little who hadn't bothered to cover his little 'sausage' was the first to recover and walked cockily halfway up the hall towards Celia.

'No problem Celia, we'll take a five-minute break, is that OK folks?' And he sauntered off to the kitchen.

Celia grabbed Aunty Pat's arm and dragged her back out the front door.

'Bastard! I'll cook his sausage for him, stamp club indeed! Humph!'

'Celia! I was enjoying that, I haven't had such a laugh since Steve Lanky bent over to pick up a fiver that had fallen out of his pocket in the butcher's. Well you know these ere new five pounds notes are like plastic, they don't bend and this one pinged out and onto the floor,' Aunty Pat stopped for a chuckle.

'For goodness sake Aunty Pat, get to the important bit,' Celia said impatiently.

'Well that's what happened see, we saw his important bits, coz his trousers split and he was doing commander,' Aunty Pat dissolved into laughter, crossed her legs, and carried on, 'Oh my, I'm gonna wet me drawers in a minute.'

'Aunty Pat, you are a one, come on let's get these costumes in the store room,' Celia said.

'Oh yes, yes, yes, I'll take these Celia,' Auntie Pat said and picking up a bundle of costumes rushed back into the hall.

Oh Lord, I hope Aunty Pat doesn't have high blood pressure, Celia thought as she grabbed the remainder of the costumes and followed her into the hall. Much to Celia's amusement, Aunty Pat hadn't made it as far as the store room, she had stopped outside the kitchen door and was trying to make conversation with anybody brave enough to make eye contact. Celia looked around and found her prey, Angela fishing Baker. Celia smiled as she approached her, like a crocodile stalking a particularly tasty frog. The poor woman didn't stand a chance, even though she pretended to be doing something on her phone.

'What Ho Angela! And where are you going to pop that phone when you restart your ping-pong?' Celia passed by pushing Auntie Pat in front of her, and they took the costumes into the store room. Once they'd put the clothes down the two women doubled up with laughter, Aunty Pat crossing her legs.

'It's no good I've got to have a wee, but I don't want to bump into a naked woman,' Aunty Pat said.

'Well go in the gents then, coz you won't mind bumping in to one of the men,' Celia replied, still silently laughing.

'As long as it's not Little John,' said Aunty Pat and burst out laughing which set Celia off, 'Oh bugger, I've wee'd myself a little bit,' Aunty Pat said, which set them off again.

'Eergh erm! If you ladies have finished we'd like to get on with our game. If you remember Celia we have booked the hall and we are paying for it.' John Little said pompously, standing with his arms folded in the store room doorway trying to look disapproving, but that's a hard look to pull off when you are naked in front of two women who aren't.

'We've finished now, so we'll get out of your way. Yes, John I do remember, you booked the hall for your stamp collecting club I believe you told us in writing? Come on Aunty Pat,' Celia said and hustled Aunty Pat in front of her.

There was a tricky moment when John Little realised that Aunty Pat was going to try and squeeze past him in the doorway. She moves fast for an old lady he thought as he jumped clear of the door. Celia propelled Aunty Pat from behind right through the hall and out the door the other end.

'I need a cup of tea after that,' said Aunty Pat.

'I need a gin,' replied Celia. 'It's not that I'm a prude. If they want to play naked table tennis I don't personally have a problem with it, but it's the fact that he lied. It will still have to be approved by the Parish Hall committee and there would have to be a few guidelines in place as well, such as keeping the curtains closed and the most important of all, not sitting on the new hall chairs with naked buttocks!'

'Git in girl and I'll drive us back to yours,' Aunty Pat ordered Celia.

Knowing what Auntie Pat's driving was like Celia hesitated but didn't want to offend so went and stood by the passenger door of the old red Peugeot, waiting for her to unlock it.

'It bain't locked, them rascally great grandchildren of mine been playing in em and broke the locks,' Aunty Pat said.

'Oh dear, aren't you worried someone might steal it?' asked Celia.

'Bless, who's going to steal my ole car, everyone knows it's Aunty Pats,' she said.

Celia climbed in and went down quite a long way before her bottom connected with the seat. Her eyes were level with the glove box which with Aunty Pat's driving was probably a good thing. She thought Aunty Pat was probably being a bit naive to think as she did, times were changing and there were a lot of new people moving in but when Celia looked at the state of the car, she thought it probably didn't matter. Aunty Pat climbed in and assumed her usual driving position, almost horizontal. Celia still hadn't quite got used to her driving whilst looking through the steering wheel but hoped as it wasn't far and it was through the village, the journey would be slow as Aunty Pat would want to wave to everybody she knew as she drove through like the queen giving the royal wave.

Curious Cat

C at, trundling along the lane in her bright yellow van like a psychedelic version of Postman Pat but without the cat, was thinking about her night ahead with Sharon as noticed she was approaching the drive to Stonepark. She was thinking it was funny to think one of her ancestors had lived there, certainly not as the Lady of the Manor but as a scullery maid. Poor Edna, what a shit life Cat thought, scullery maid, assistant to the kitchen maid. Her long days would have been spent scouring the plates, pots, crocks, stove and the floor. She would also have had to scrub the vegetables, pluck the fowls and scale the fish. Before the cook arrived in the kitchen in the morning, Edna's first tasks in the morning would be lighting the stoves and fetching and boiling the water for tea and washing and all for her keep and about six pounds a year. Cat felt sorry for her but wished she'd had a different name to the one which had been passed down to the females in the family.

Along with her name, the story of the mysterious disappearance of Edna had also been passed down.

As she got closer to Stonepark, Cat noticed some activity. There were men standing around the door of the house and a lorry. What a good opportunity, she thought. If the owners are around I can introduce myself. I might gain some new clients, everyone needs a hairdresser. She pulled in at the top of the drive, turned the engine off, and leaving the van, walked down the grass on the side of the drive. She couldn't see anyone when she reached the lorry but the front door was open and she could hear a murmuring of voices, the men must have moved indoors. I'll take just a little peek she thought, as she approached the lorry, see what sort of furniture they have. At the back of the lorry, she looked inside the darkened interior. The nearest thing to her was huge, it went from floor to the roof of the lorry and was wrapped in giant bubble-wrap. She dug her nail into the plastic but it was strong and wouldn't break, she pulled a pencil from her pocket and dug that in but it was too thick. She jumped up into the lorry for a better look and then she could see the outline and feel that it was a large stone fireplace. Suddenly, she heard gravel crunching from her left. She didn't want to be caught snooping, so jumping down she turned and walked briskly around the opposite side of the van straight into the chest of a giant.

Not Quite the Full Monty

❧

L ilac stepped out of her front door and wondered how she was going to attract Monty's attention. He was cutting her grass and wouldn't be able to hear her over the noise of the motor. She would have to physically touch him. She hadn't done that yet. Monty turned just as she reached out a hand to tap him on his back and her hand met the hard muscle of his chest. The sensation travelled all the way to a place that hadn't been fired up in a long time.

'Sorry, sorry, I wanted to tell you I'm popping to the library van, Harold has ordered a book for me. You look hot, I mean you must be hot, help yourself to a drink or I could...'

'Lilac, stop, breathe, go get your book. We'll have a cold drink together when I've finished,' Monty said as he smiled at her.

Already flustered, his devastating smile didn't help. Lilac hurried off to fetch her book hoping the light breeze would cool her hot cheeks. As she walked along Monty filled her thoughts. He had been coming around now for a few weeks, ever since Nathan had left. He would carry her shopping from the boot of her car into the house, sometimes he would call around and they would sit in the garden and share a bottle of beer that he had brought with him. When he started cutting her grass for her once a week it wasn't long before after he'd finished they would sit and chat over a cup of tea. He was very funny and made her laugh. She thought she had laughed more in the short time she had known Monty than in the whole of her seven years with Nathan the Bastard. She thanked the day when fate stepped in and she saw the photograph that exposed her ex for what he was, a cheating, lying bastard.

She couldn't believe how quickly Nathan had faded from her mind and her heart and how she fast she was falling for Monty. She wasn't a kid, she'd known from the beginning that he fancied her, but she also knew that she wasn't ready for a new relationship, especially not that quick after breaking up with Nathan. Monty had been the perfect gentleman and they had formed a strong friendship but to her surprise, oh, how she wanted that to change. It was madness she knew, but she was so drawn to him and felt she had known him for ages, it was becoming physical torture to be close to him. With Monty there always seemed to be something to talk about, they were both history lovers and he was full of knowledge about architecture and different periods and styles. She'd found out he was also a keen gardener and he'd shared with Lilac stories about his Gran and Grandad's allotment, where he had spent a lot of time as a child whilst his parents were working. Although they always seemed to have plenty of things to talk about, and shared similar views on many things, she didn't know very much about him personally. She knew she was falling in love and she was frightened. Monty was only here to do a job, she knew that much, and he was lodging at the Unfurled Moth. When the job finished he would be gone.

Monty had seemed a bit distracted today she thought, there seemed to be something troubling him. Perhaps he was about to move on and didn't know how to tell her. But then, he didn't have to tell her, it's not as if they were in a relationship, they were just friends. If he was leaving she knew she would miss him terribly. She had tried to keep her feelings in check, knowing she was vulnerable, but apart from the fact he was freaking gorgeous, he made her laugh, and they were friends. She hurried along to the library van. She hoped Harold wasn't in a chatty mood because she wanted to pick up her book and get back to Monty.

Monty watched until Lilac had gone, then he stripped off his t-shirt and started up the mower. He enjoyed working in the garden, he'd missed it and he was pleased to be able to help Lilac with hers for more reasons than one. He couldn't stop thinking about Stonepark. He was ashamed at the work he and his crew had carried out. When Max had offered him the job in Devon the money was too good to refuse and he was happy to get out of London for a while. It all seemed perfect until he'd actually visited Stonepark, then he was horrified at the destruction of an amazing house. It didn't matter that they were putting replacement fireplaces in, the originals should have remained in place. He was glad that the Russian's men had taken over and he didn't have to take the last fireplace out. What he wanted to do was stay here in St Urith and pursue the luscious Lilac, but if anyone found out what he and his crew had done at Stonepark who, knew what would happen? He'd bet his halfpenny he'd not be welcome in the village. More than that, he worried about his future relationship with Lilac. He knew how hurt she had been about her ex and his lies, she wouldn't tolerate dishonesty from anyone again. Could he put it right? Could he at least stop that last magnificent fireplace from being taken?

Cat in Crisis

'Get your hands off me you ape!' shouted Cat as she kicked back against her captor's shins. Unfortunately, she only had flip-flops on and they slipped off her feet. She kicked with her heels but it didn't have any effect.

'Calm down little lady, there's no need to be frightened, if you calm down he'll let you go,' Max told her.

'Calm down, you idiot? Would you calm down if some big ape grabbed you and dragged you away? Now let go of me!' Cat shouted.

'Now, now little lady...'

'Little Lady? What century are you living in? Now tell your monkey to put me down, you are all going to be in big trouble, you can't go around grabbing women!' Cat shouted at Max.

'OK, OK, I'm sorry, I apologise for calling you a little lady but...'

'Oh, that's bloody brilliant, bloody priceless you

are, you're apologising for calling me little lady when your goon has assaulted me and is holding me two foot off the effing floor!' Cat screamed the last word, causing Max to wince.

'Oh, you stupid girl, stop shouting and screaming, you are only going to make things worse. You've got to calm down, I'm not in charge here, I'm trying to help you,' Max pleaded, worried as to what the Russians would do with the girl. He was beginning to wish he hadn't come back to Stonewall to finish things off. He still didn't know what had happened to the other chap they'd found snooping around and he damn sure he didn't want to. All he wanted was to get this job finished, get paid and get out of there, this was getting all too heavy for his liking. He had never been involved in violence and he was frightened for himself and for the girl.

Cat sensed that what Max was saying had an element of truth to it, he looked frightened and obviously had no control over the giant who was holding her.

'OK, I'm calm, now tell this idiot to put me down, I won't shout or scream anymore,' Cat said.

'Put her down, she can't go anywhere the doors are all locked,' Max said to the man who was behind Cat in the shadows of the kitchen.

Cat hadn't seen the other man from where she was held suspended in the air. She turned her head to try and see but couldn't. The other man said something unintelligible but sounded like Russian, and Cat was dropped onto the flagstone floor of the kitchen. She landed awkwardly and her ankle turned under her.

'Oh, shit that hurts! You bastard! You've broken my ankle!' Cat rubbed at her rapidly swelling ankle, tears in her eyes.

'Oh, I'm so sorry, wait there a second,' Max said, solicitously.

'Hah, very funny,' Cat said defiantly from where she sat on the floor, but she was scared and in pain and couldn't stop the tears that ran down her cheeks.

Max knelt on the floor next to her and gently examined her foot.

'I don't think it's broken, I think it's a bad sprain. This should make it feel a bit easier,' Max wrapped a cold wet tea-towel carefully around her foot, then held out a glass of water and a packet of Paracetamol.

'Enough of the nursing Max, this is yet another little problem that we have to clear up,' said the second man, angrily.

'What are you all doing here anyway? This house belongs to Lady Marigold's mother, and what was all that stuff doing in the van? This is a listed building, you are grave-robbers that's what you are, you won't get away with it!' Cat said.

'Grave-robbers? No, no, my dear, you are completely wrong, because this house has been bought by my client and you are trespassing. So, I think you had better leave, don't you? Now let me help you up,' Max said, looking at the girl meaningfully, hoping she would catch on. He was thinking quickly, he needed to get the girl out before the Russian goons realised how much she knew. Carefully, he pulled her to her feet and walked her hobbling towards the door. Cat was not a stupid girl and she quickly realised that Max was trying to get her out of there. His reaction wasn't the normal one of someone finding a stranger in their drive and asking them to leave, he genuinely looked frightened for her.

'Oh dear, I am so sorry, what an idiot I've made of myself,' Cat started to limp towards the door holding on to Max's arm.

'That's OK my dear, no harm done, no need to mention it to anyone, my client likes to protect his privacy,' Max said to Cat as they neared the door.

'I don't think so,' A voice said from behind them.

Max and Cat had just reached the door and Max went to lift the latch but the talking Russian pushed in front of it.

'I said I don't think so Max. Now take the girl over there and sit her down on the floor.'

'Step away Boris, I'm leaving and I'm not a girl, I'm a woman and you can't keep me here against my will,' Cat objected.

'Patya, please, let the girl go, she doesn't know anything, 'Max pleaded.

'Bogdan, take the girl and put her in the corner,' Patya ordered.

The big Russian, Bogdan, who resembled a tree, picked Cat up as if she weighed no more than a small child.

'Get off me you big ape! Ow, you're hurting me, let me go or you'll be sorry,' Cat struggled but it was like trying to move a steel cage and she was dumped down in the corner of the kitchen in the recess next to the fireplace.

Cat was frightened. She had no idea what was going on or what she had stepped into but realised that she was in a very dangerous situation and that nobody knew where she was. Max wouldn't be able to help her, he'd already tried and failed. It was clear the Russians were in control of whatever was going on here. She felt as if she was in a film set but a horror movie, it was so unreal. Although she tried hard to keep control of her emotions, she couldn't help the tears that fell. She looked across the bare kitchen at Max who silently mouthed 'I'm sorry' to her.

Lilac in Lust

Lilac hurried away from the library clutching the book in her arms. There was no sign of Monty in her front garden when she arrived home and she felt a wave of disappointment wash over her. He must have gone back to the Unfurled Moth. Then, to her delight, she heard the sound of the mower coming from the back garden. She quickly let herself in, put the book down on the kitchen counter and went out the back door. Oh, what a vision met her eyes as she stepped into the garden. Monty, bare chested, was bending down taking off the grass box from the back of the mower. He walked to the garden fence, tipped the grass into the field and turned, stopping dead when he saw Lilac and dropped the empty grass box. Watching the trickle of sweat run down his chest to his navel, her eyes followed it as it slid down the line of hair that disappeared into his low slung linen shorts. She saw his physical reaction, it was fast and obvious and she felt an answering throbbing response in her own body. Her limbs felt weak, she couldn't move, didn't want to. Monty dropped the grass box and moved towards her slowly, where she stood waiting. He could see in her eyes she wanted him as much as he wanted her. He picked her up and walked through the bungalow, into her bedroom where he lay her down like a precious object, gently on the bed.

'Are you sure Lilac? I know I am, I've wanted you since the first time I saw you. I love you, but you've just come out of a relationship and I don't want...'

'Shut up and kiss me,' demanded Lilac, pulling him down on top of her.

The Ring of Light

Ronald was set for the evening with a glass of Cote du Rhone and a book to read. He was sat on the other side of the room from Celia. The reason for not sitting on the sofa in his usual spot next to Celia was because she was knitting with a giant pair of wooden knitting needles and some strips of Welsh blanket which she was knitting into a bedside rug. The needles were so large that every now and again he would get a clonk in a tender area from the hard, wooden end of the needle and he'd got fed up with it and moved away. Thank goodness Celia seemed to have calmed down and got over all that nonsense about that Max chappie, Ronald thought. When she gets a bee in her bonnet there is no stopping her. I know she's thinking he is up to something with that other chap, but now she's engrossed with her knitting and watching an Agatha Christie perhaps she will let it drop.

'Sounds like the Air Ambulance Ronald,' Celia

said. They had large picture windows all around their sitting room and could see lots of sky, but you generally heard things before you saw them and it was surprising how long it took to find them in the vastness of the sky. She looked out the window but couldn't see anything from where she sat, anyway it was quite dark. The sound got louder and even Ronald who was hard of hearing heard it.

'I hear it, think it's coming this way and it's fairly low, better get out there with the lights just in case,' Ronald said.

As fast as they could manage they hurried around to the playing field. There were quite a few people already there when they arrived, including Betty, Dusty and Lilac. Willie arrived with his eggshell candelabra lantern. He'd obviously come out in a hurry because all he was wearing, apart from a tombstone grin, was a grubby set of long Johns of indeterminate colour. The bottoms were predictably held up with baler twine and one unwanted sleeve was attached to Willie's head like a surreal nightcap. Fred came along just behind Willie and soon there was a circle of light around the landing spot.

'It's just like that film isn't it Celia?' asked Ronald.

'What film?' Celia responded.

'That kid's film, you know the one.'

'Ronald, there are millions of kid's films, I have no idea what film you mean.'

'Hang on, I remember it's Elton John, I love a bit of Elton.'

'Do you mean Kingsman? Elton was in that.'

'I've got it, it's an animated one, a Disney, The Ring of Light, the one with all the lions in,' Ronald said triumphantly.

Luckily, Celia didn't have to answer as the helicopter was approaching and the noise of it made all talking impossible but she gave Ronald a look. However, as they all looked up it wasn't the Devon Air Ambulance, it was a sleek shiny helicopter, black with a custom design along the side. The crowd didn't know what to think except that perhaps the Devon Air Ambulance had broken down and this was a replacement helicopter, but it was pretty swish. There was lots of speculation amongst the crowd but the noise was so loud they couldn't talk about it. The helicopter came to rest and as soon as the blades slowed to a stop the circle of villagers closed in. The door flew open and two large men dressed in black suits, with crisp white shirts, black ties and dark sunglasses stepped out and stood one either side of the doorway.

'Oh my, it's the MIB,' said Dusty.

'Who's the MIB?' asked Betty.

'You know, the 'Men in Black' the Will Smith films with the aliens.'

Willie stepped up closer to them with his strange egg-shade candelabra.

'You dree's a right pair, if you want to stay yer, you better get out. Caw, 'tis a mort'l size I tell 'ee, me boody, I eb'm zin nort like it,' Willie said impressed.

'That be a Eurocopter EC130B4, an ee's bootiful,' informed Eric Beech.

Celia, who hadn't understood a word Willie had said, but was stood next to Eric was impressed.

'Wow I didn't know you were an expert on Helicopters Eric. By the way where is Tommy?'

'I don't know Celia, and I'm worried. He went off to put up the poster about the bell ringing tour and then he was gwain to walk Daisy as usual, I haven't seen im' since,' Eric said, clearly upset.

'Ee never come 'ome and we always 'ave a game a snooker after tea but ee never come 'ome.'

'That does seem worrying. Don't worry Eric, there are a lot of us here, I'm sure that some of us will help you look for him, once we've finished here,' Celia said.

The Hon Sharon who was the other side of Ronald, much to his pleasure, had been listening to this conversation and spoke to Celia.

'Celia, Cat is missing too. I hope I'm not being overly dramatic, I wouldn't normally worry but she would *always* let me know if she couldn't make our date. She's not answering her phone and I have phoned around to everywhere I thought she might be and I cannot find her. I have this terrible feeling that there is something wrong,' this last sentence was a sob from Sharon.

Just then a third figure jumped out of the helicopter. The man was tall and slim, wearing a dark grey well fitted suit with a paler grey roll-neck jumper underneath. His dark hair was cut very short, like bristles on his head and his very light bluish grey eyes were quite startling. Standing between the first two men he looked around at the circle of villagers, and then in astonishment at Willie.

'Where the hell am I and who are you and all these people? Where is Max?' the man asked.

'You'm like a tawd 'n a bucket, ee be praper maized Fred,' Willie said and chortled to himself.

'Ee' don't know where ee be,' Willie thought it hilarious.

The man said something to his two men and they both moved and stepped in between him and Willie.

'You'm a couple of big buggers, bain't ee, bet 'ee eats a lot 'o eggs,' Willie said looking up at the men and grinning.

The third man pulled out his mobile phone and started speaking rapidly into it.

'He's a Russian Ronald, what would a Russian be doing landing a private and obviously very expensive helicopter in St Urith?' Celia asked, 'and I'm sure I heard amongst that gobbledygook the name Max.'

'I don't know what he's doing here Celia, but if he's Russian and can afford what is one and a half million pounds worth of helicopter he's what they call an Oligarch and those others are his minders.' Ronald replied.

The Russian put away his phone and turned to climb back into the helicopter.

'Where be gwain me boody? If 'eed 'ev asked me I could o' told 'ee 'ee wuz lost!' Willie called out.

To everyone's surprise, the Russian stopped before he climbed into the helicopter. He turned around and pushing between the minders he came face to face with Willie. Well, not actually face to face, Willie being a good forty plus centimeters shorter. The Russian snapped his finger and pointed to Willie, the minders moved one either side of Willie and were clearly expected to lift him up by the arms to the oligarch's level. But when they got close, Willie's natural aroma and one arm made the manoeuvre smellier and trickier than they had anticipated. The Oligarch shouted at them in Russian, they looked at each other and came to a silent agreement. Bending down they each grasped a grubby trousered leg just below Willie's knees and lifted him, still in a standing position. They raised him up until he was level with the Oligarch.

'Yay hey!' Willie shouted as he went up in the air, he was having a brilliant time, then as his face came level with the Russian, he shouted,

'Ow be you my luvver, wer be gwain? can I ave a ride in thicky gurt big bird?'

'What language are you speaking?' the Russian asked Willie.'

''Ee be a praper bleddy doughbake buy, this be Nor' Debben, God's own country,' Willie replied.

The Russian shook his head, turned, and climbed into the helicopter and the minders lowered Willie down to the ground and walked to the helicopter door. The two men didn't get in, but both sniffed their hands and seemed to be having some sort of discussion. Then they both took off their jackets, sniffed the edges of the sleeves and folded them outside in and stuffed them under the seat nearest the door of the helicopter. One of them pulled out a hand sanitizer sprayed both his hands and passed it to his colleague who did the same and then both vigorously rubbing their hands together they climbed in. Within seconds of the door closing the helicopter rose up into the air and headed off. Most of the villagers went home but Celia had spread the word about Cat and Tommy and asked for volunteers to stay and work out where they could start searching.

'Betty, do you think you could pop home for some Bin Gin? I'm not sure what is going to happen tonight but I think we'd all do better for a restorative and I think Bin Gin is just what is needed. I have my key to the Parish Hall, let's all go inside and then when Betty comes back we can decide what we are going to do,' Celia suggested. She unlocked the doors and they all trooped inside, Ronald flipping on the lights.

Proper Job

M ax meanwhile, having taken an earful of abuse from the Oligarch on his mobile phone, had run to his beloved Jaguar and had driven it off the drive and onto the edge of the huge lawn on the Dartmoor side of Stonepark. Leaving his engine running and his headlights on, he ran to find the other lamps that he had left dotted about the lawn and switched them on, he could hear the helicopter coming. The helicopter landed on the lawn of Stonepark, the two muscle men climbed out followed by their boss. Max rushed forward to greet him.

'What is this place? There are no lights! How are you expected to find anywhere in this darkness? Things have gone bad Max, so everything here must be 100%. We were guided in by landing lights, which we thought were yours. I thought I'd landed in some sort of asylum but it wasn't, it was in a village near here and there was a crazy little man who speak in a strange language.

Everything here is good?' Without waiting for a reply the Oligarch carried on, 'One hundred percent, Max, that's what I'm looking for, I don't want troubles, I want to use this house in the future and I don't want troubles with the people here. Have all the specified pieces been removed and packed ready to ship?' asked the Russian.

'Ship? Nobody mentioned ship before, it doesn't say in the paperwork they are being transported by ship? Anyway, I don't think you would get all the way up the river Torridge to here in a ship, you might up the Taw but that's too far away. It's all been loaded into the lorry,' gabbled Max.

'You idiotic man! Show me the lorry,' the Oligarch ordered.

Max was so strung out with stress that if you'd have run your fingers over him, you could have played 'Great Balls of Fire!' He was frightened of what the Oligarchs reaction would be when he discovered Cat and Tommy. Never in his career as a small time con-man had he been involved in violence and he couldn't handle it. He decided that if he got the chance he would make his escape, with or without the money, before anything more went wrong. Max led the Oligarch around the house to where the lorry was parked and the Russian climbed up into the back of lorry and, using a high powered torch, inspected the bubble wrapped pieces one by one.

'Good, good, your man has done well, the pieces are perfect, now we inspect the replacements.'

Max and the Oligarch moved through the house

from room to room inspecting the replacement fireplaces fitted by Monty and his team.

'This is a good job Max,' the Oligarch said slapping him on the back and nearly knocking him off his feet as they headed towards the kitchen.

'Saving the best to last, the one in the kitchen is my wife's favourite, it is to go in the room with the swimming pool with the statues, it will look good, yes?' asked the Oligarch.

'Oh yes, absolutely 'proper job' as they say here in Devon,' Max replied with an embarrassed little laugh.

'Of course, it will be a proper job, idiot!' the Oligarch was not amused.

Max's heart sank, the last thing he wanted was to antagonise this man and he certainly didn't want the Oligarch to enter the kitchen and discover Cat and Tommy because he had a horrible feeling that something unthinkable might happen to them. If he could assure the Oligarch that everything was done as per his instructions, keep him out of the kitchen and get him back to his helicopter, then he could let them both go, leave himself and get the hell out of Devon.

'Your wife quite clearly has exquisite taste, and what a clever idea to use that particular fireplace as a seat, and as for the statues, well the Poseidon statue is a stroke of genius,' Max said.

'Hmm... you haven't met my wife have you? I didn't marry her for her genius, she is very beautiful woman and I do not require her to think. I employed a designer to tell her what she wanted and she wanted these fireplaces in our new house which will be a home to impress. It is where we entertain the rich and the famous and my house must be more beautiful and more impressive than theirs.'

'Well, you have seen everything now, I'll show you the way back to your helicopter and I'll make sure the lorry gets off promptly and I'll clean everything up here and lock up. I promise you that you can safely leave everything in my hands,' Max gabbled, words tumbling over each other with the intent of reassuring the Russian and getting him out of the house. Max put a hand behind the Russian's back as if to steer him away from the kitchen.

The Russian stopped and gave Max a look that could churn butter and he swiftly dropped his arm.

'Are you trying to get rid of me Max? Is there something that you do not want me to see in the kitchen?'

'No, no, of course not, it's only Patya and Bogdan tidying everything up. I just know what a busy man you are and as you said previously it is very dark out there and I didn't want you to get lost trying to find your helicopter...' Max's voice petered out at the sceptical look from the Russian.

Pushing his way through the kitchen door the oligarch stopped as he saw Cat and Tommy, hands tied, sitting in the alcove next to the newly fitted replacement fireplace. Petrya and Bogdar were standing guard.

'You have caused big problems Max, two big problems. Who are these problems? What are they doing here? I am sure that you remember my original instructions, that this project was to be strictly top-secret, undercover, covert, confidential, need I go on? The Russian spoke quietly but somehow to Max's ears more threateningly.

'Er with all due respect, you do realise that your house is in the parish of St Urith With Well?' Max asked.

'Idiot! I bought this house of course I know where it is. What is this Urith's Well?

'It's the name of this Parish, it's the same name as the village and I have to tell you that these small Devon villages are worse than your KGB. They know what you've done before you've done it. Me and my team have not told a soul about anything to do with this house, these two were just nosy and came to see what we were doing here,' Max continued, 'they would have gone away without any problems and we would have been out of here without any unpleasantness, but your two Neanderthals grabbed them, manhandled them and wouldn't let them go. And that my friend, is assault and kidnap and I didn't sign up for violence!' Max crossed his arms as he finished speaking on a bit of a high note as he had worked himself up into a temper, a combination of fear and anger.

'Shut up, you silly little man with your oh so English airs and graces,' the Russian said then turned to his men. There was a lot of gesticulating and excited chatter then the Oligarch turned to Max.

'Your job here is done.' He pulled out a large packet from his inside jacket pocket and handed it to Max.

'You are finished, you can go, we will clear up your mess here and I suggest you get out of Devon as soon as you can, preferably tonight.' Turning his back on Max he looked at his two captives sitting on the floor across the room.

Cat was terrified, she felt like she was in the middle of a nightmare but she was awake and it was all too real, as the pain from her wrists and shoulders confirmed. When the man who had come in with Max looked across at her, she felt her insides turn to jelly, her head began to swim and she thought she would faint. Not religious in any way Cat still found herself looking up to the ceiling, then closing her eyes, silently asking for help. She opened her eyes just as a beautiful pure white feather floated down from the ceiling, she opened and cupped her bound hands enough for the feather to fall in and in a small way felt comforted. Max watched the feather fall into the young woman's hands and knew he had to make another attempt to rescue them both. There was a bit of him that thought that he was overreacting, things like this don't really happen in real life, but overriding this was the fear that if he left them here with the Russians something terrible would happen to the hapless pair and they might disappear. No, I'm being ridiculous, people don't get murdered like that in real life, especially in rural Devon, but can I take that chance? Max looked across at the terrified Cat and Eric (Tommy) and decided that he would make one more attempt to rescue them, he didn't want them on his conscience when he left Devon. He put on his jolly English chappie persona.

'Righto, thanks for that, I'll pop along now. Come along you two, I'll drop you both off on my way home.'

Cat and Tommy struggled to their feet, not easy with your hands tied. Luckily, they were tied at the front and not at the back which would have been excruciating. They both tentatively walked towards Max but didn't get very far before the oligarch spoke.

'They will stay. Now I suggest that you go Max, while you have the chance. Or perhaps you would like to remain with your friends?'

Max gave Cat and Eric (Tommy) a last look and left, trying to convince himself that they would be fine, that the Russian was bound to let them go, nobody was murdered over a few fireplaces!

Cat sat back down on the floor. She had been trying hard not to cry but now her tears fell freely. She had put her faith in Max, after all he had tried to save them once, but perhaps he would go for help. That's all she could hope, but she wasn't sure how long they'd have. When she looked at the Oligarch, he looked like a Russian villain in a James Bond Movie. The two Russian heavies were talking animatedly to the Oligarch. They stopped abruptly and one of them went to the side of the large fireplace and started fiddling around. There was an audible click and the Russian swung the whole of the fireplace out showing a gap of about fort- three centimetres. They were smiling and chatting, obviously pleased with themselves, slapping each other on the back and shoulder bumping when they were stopped abruptly by some harsh words from their boss. The two thugs grabbed Cat and threw her into the gaping black space behind the fireplace, followed by Tommy. Then the fireplace was pushed back into place.

Maid in the Dark

❧❧❧

Cat was frozen to the spot where she had stumbled. She was alone and terrified. It was so dark, not a chink of light penetrated the thick cloying blackness. Helpless, she could feel the panic rising as her breaths came in gasps, a sob rising on a breath of air.

'There maid, there there,' a soft gentle voice spoke from somewhere in front of her.

'It's me, Tommy, don't 'ee worry maid, we'll be alright,' Tommy said and reached a hand forward until he found Cat's and held on tight.

'Oh Tommy, don't let go, please don't let go, I can't breathe, we're going to die, oh God!' Cat was panicking.

'Shs, shss Cat, try and stay calm maid, we'll be alright, be outa' 'ere in no time.

Cat forced herself to calm down, she breathed deeply in and out, in and out.

'But how Tommy? Nobody knows we are in here

and there can't be much air in here, we'll suffoate! Oh God!' Cat started to cry again.

'Hush little maid, we've plenty o' air, this be one o' they priest holes and they wouldn't want to kill a priest, they were saving them. Anyway, people will come looking for us soon, I know ole' Eric will be looking for me. I aven't missed snooker with 'im fer these past thirty yers.' He patted Cat's arm comfortingly but secretly thought the same, that the air wouldn't last long in this airtight tomb.

Celia in Command

B ack in the parish hall, Celia looked around at the familiar faces. There was Ronald of course, the Hon Sharon, Eric Beech, Harold, Betty, Dusty, Lilac, Fred and Willie. She raised her fat measure of Bin Gin.

'Well my friends, whatever happens tonight, we're in it together, bottoms up!'

At that moment the door burst open and Aunty Pat walked in.

'What be dwain my lovers?' asked Aunty Pat, 'ave I missed a party?'

'Don't ee look a picture,' Betty complimented Aunty Pat on her new hair colour, 'that be a luverly shade, it do suit you a treat my dear.'

Ronald hastily fetched a glass from the kitchen, gave it to her, went to fill it and then stopped, asking, 'Are you driving Aunty Pat?'

'Do I bleddy look like it?'

She shoved the glass under Ronald's nose and he

decided she was old enough to decide for herself if she was going to drive or not, besides he wasn't brave enough to refuse her a Bin Gin. Ronald rolled his eyes at Celia who shrugged but didn't say anything, so he filled Aunty Pat's glass up without another word.

'How did you know we were in here Aunty Pat?' asked Celia.

'I had an email saying lights be on in the Parish Hall and Betty been seed taking 'er Bin Gin in, so I thought to meself, I is a bit creaky tonight, I could do with a medicinal and 'ere I am,' with that Aunty Pat tipped her glass up and swallowed the lot.

'Right, now, where were we... There's something going on in St Urith, I'm not sure what it is but I have a feeling that Russian is something to do with it. I mean, don't you think it's bizarre that a million-pound helicopter with three Russians on board lands in our playing field in St Urith?'

'One and a half million, elicopter.'

'Yes, thank you Eric. It's not improbable that Cat and Tommy are caught up in it somehow. That Russian came here tonight for a reason and he definitely mentioned Max's name. I think that Max Cheetham and that Monty are in it up to their necks!' Celia said excitedly.

'I don't think Monty would get involved in something bad, he's a really good bloke,' Lilac protested.

'Well, if he's a good bloke as you say he is, go and fetch him. Then we'll ask him what he and Max and the Russians are up to,' asked Celia, 'I think if put all the facts that we know or suspect together, we might come up with some ideas. You start Harold, tell them about the piece of paper you found,' Celia said.

'Ergh erm, would it be alright if I joined in? I think I have some information that could help,' asked a voice. They all turned to find Monty. He'd met Lilac at the door of the hall as she was leaving to fetch him. They walked in and stood in the circle, his arm protectively around Lilac.

Ronald ran to fetch another glass for Monty but before he could hand it over Celia stopped him.

'I don't think we should be cozying up to him Ronald!'

Lilac stepped forward and took it from Ronald saying, 'Fill it up Ronald, we are sharing.'

'You and that Max Cheetham are up to something dodgy, aren't you? Don't try and deny it, I know you are. Our priority now is to find Cat and Tommy. It's too much of a coincidence that they have both gone missing. Sharon was meant to be meeting up with Cat and she wouldn't let her down without calling to explain why, and Eric says that there is no way Tommy would miss his snooker and he has never stayed out this late from walking Daisy. That Russian who just landed his helicopter here in the village is something to do with it isn't he? I heard him mention Max's name, and anybody who can afford a luxury helicopter is splashing the cash.'

'Splashing the cash? Where did you get that expression from Celia? You've been reading too many crime novels,' Ronald said.

Celia carried on, ignoring what Ronald said completely, but giving him a withering look. She'd completely forgotten she still had her knitting in her hands with her giant wooden knitting needles. She had rushed out to assist the Devon Air Ambulance and hadn't put them down. Unfortunately for Monty she was a great gesticulator and the giant wooden needles were flying about menacingly as she spoke.

'Monty if you have any idea where they might be or what might have happened to them, then you had better tell us right now!'

As Celia said this, she had moved closer to Monty and her voice had got shriller and louder. The last few words were shouted and Celia's pair of giant wooden knitting needles with a large ball of Welsh blanket stuck on the end with trailing bits like a hobby craft version of a Medieval 'Morning Star' were pointed close to his face.

'Celia, calm down. You can't shout and accuse someone without proof like that, and put those needles down!' Ronald said to Celia and he took the arm with the knitting needles and tried to pull her away. Celia was furious and through gritted teeth said to Ronald,

'Don't tell me to calm down, saying that just makes me angrier than I was in the first place!' yelled Celia using the needles to make her point. She took a deep breath to calm herself but her inner turmoil over Cat and Tommy rolled around her stomach like a fried egg sandwich. She turned to Monty.

'But I'm not wrong am I Monty? This is all to do with this Russian, Ronald says he's an Oligarch. I'm guessing he's funding whatever it is you are up to with Max Cheetham.'

'Celia, you have no right to shout at Monty like that, he's done nothing wrong,' Lilac said, ready to defend him.

'It's OK Lilac, she's right, let her speak,' Monty put an arm around Lilac's shoulders and hugged her to him.

'My guess is that you are, more or less, an honest man but somehow or other you have got mixed up in something very wrong with that Max chappie. Am I right?' Celia asked Monty.

Before he could answer the Hon Sharon burst out, 'Oh for goodness sake! Forget all that, what about Cat? She must be in trouble, we've got to go and find her now!'

'I know you're anxious my dear, but we don't want to go off all half-cocked. I think we need to look at all the clues first and listen to what Monty has to say and then we will have a better chance of finding Cat, and probably Tommy,' Celia said.

'And Daisy,' Eric said.

'Yes of course, Eric and Daisy,' Celia confirmed.

'That's what the kids at school used to call 'ee alf-cock,' sniggered Wille. He wiggled his shoulders from side to side and waved his one arm about, in front of the ladies.

'See 'alf-cock, git it, I'm a Cock and there be on'y 'alf of me,' Willie laughed and Fred and the others. All except Monty and Lilac who didn't get the joke joined in, if a little hysterically, as the tension in the room was so thick you could have cut it with a scythe.

Celia a little nervous about what she was going to say next and hoping that everyone didn't think she was going mad, carried on, 'For me, it all started with an angel, and before you all think I've gone barmy, hear me out. I've been dreaming about angels asking me for help, everywhere I go I see angels, I've even bought angel ornaments for the garden. I have a really strong feeling that an angel is asking me to do something. I don't really care whether you all believe me or not because I trust my instincts and my instincts are telling me that I need to listen to these angels and what they have been trying to tell me and I don't think it's a coincidence that Monty and Max are involved in something wrong. I think the two are connected. Now, Harold, tell us about Max Cheetham, the book and the piece of paper,' Celia asked, sticking her chin in the air and staring around at the others defying them to snigger. Swallowing the last of her Bin Gin she gestured to Ronald to fill it up again.

Betty turned to Dusty and quietly told her to go and fetch some more Bin Gin. Sharon was getting increasingly edgy. Celia had really gone for that Monty and he'd said he was going to tell them everything and then she started talking about Angels and now Harold is going to give a lecture about the library. She decided that it was all taking too long and she would make a move and go and try to find Cat herself. Moving slowly, she started to edge her way closer to the door.

'The Hon Sharon? I hope you aren't thinking of going anywhere on your own, we're all in this together and together we will go forward,' said Celia.

'You go Celia, you sound like bleddy Churchill!' Aunty Pat said, filling her own and Sharon's glass with more Bin Gin.

'Go on Harold,' Celia instructed.

'Max Cheetham borrowed a book from the mobile library about local houses and their architecture, when he returned the book, which was overdue, he left a piece of paper inside. I couldn't work out what it was about, so I showed it to Celia,' stated Harold.

'The piece of paper had measurements on it and some initials but even I couldn't work out what it was about, accept of course, to guess it possibly had something to do with a house. Later, I saw Max Cheetham with an antiques catalogue and then I found out about a spate of thefts from National Trust Homes! I think Monty will be able to enlighten us as to what's been going on,' Celia suggested.

Monty cleared his throat and stepped slightly away from Lilac.

'I know we're in a hurry but before I tell you what's been going on, I just want to say something to Lilac. Lilac I have never told you any lies. I know I 'aven't told you what I've been working on but I 'ave not lied to you. I'm 'ere now and I'm going to tell you all everyfing and 'elp you to find your friends. Though no offence to Celia, may I call you Celia?'

Celia nodded in the affirmative.

'I don't know about any angels, and I don't believe your friends disappearance is anyfing to do with Max. Look yeah, 'e is a bit of a wide boy and I fink 'e ducks and dives a bit but there is no way 'e would be involved in anything violent. From what he's told me he's a bit of posh con-man, he likes the high life and moves around a lot doing deals here and there and then 'e goes to the South of France and acts the playboy until his money's gone. '

'Fair enough Monty, but what about the robberies? And the Russian?' Celia asked.

'I don't know anything about no robberies, and I've never even met the Russian. Everything was arranged through Max. All I know is 'e's a millionaire and 'e's bought an 'ouse, down Surrey way and 'e bought this 'ouse in Devon, because 'e wanted some of the architectural features out of it. I 'ave met some of his thugs though, and they're both a nasty piece of work,' Monty paused, long enough for Willie to pipe up.

'Waz 'e saying? 'E be a propper bleddy dimwit, I don' be knowin' a bleddy word.'

'Monty comes from London Willie, he has a cockney accent,' Lilac explained.

Willie, who looked a bit like those glo-worm night-lights that children have, bald, with hats on but grubbier, and with the hat being the armless sleeve of his top, became very animated which wasn't a pretty sight.

His long-johns had long ago shrunk in the wash, whatever year that was, and there were bits of Willie moving about in quite a disturbing way, that everyone's eyes were trying to ignore.

"E be a Cock like us'n? 'E be a gooden then, there be lots of us Cocks in Churchyard,' Willie said

'Don't worry about Willie, just nod your head and agree and carry on,' said Celia.

Monty looked at Willie and gave a sort of half nod, nervous that if he got too friendly this grubby little man might want to get closer, or God forbid want to hug him. Moving back a little out of Willie's reach, but still within aroma aura, he carried on,

'I love Lilac and I want to make my home and a future in St Urith so I hope you will all forgive my unwilling part in...'

'For goodness sake Monty, save the speeches till after, just tell us what you've been up to! We've got people missing here!' interrupted Celia.

'OK, sorry,' Monty straightened up, smoothed down his tee-shirt and cleared his throat, 'I have my own business in London as an architectural salvager and I agreed to do a job for Max. The job was down 'ere in Devon and I was happy to come down 'ere for a few months. I 'ave an excellent manager to run my business and I only had to return to London if there was a problem that 'e couldn't deal with,' Monty said.

Celia, impatient, cleared her throat, 'Monty, you are not being interviewed by Matt Allright for 'Rogue Traders,' tell us about the job?'

'The job was to remove some statues, pillars and fireplaces from a property owned by the Russian millionaire. They were to be replaced wiv some new stone fireplaces in keeping with the property and the originals to be taken to the Surrey property that the Russian owned, where he had experts waiting to fit them,' Monty said.

'That don't sound like a crime to me,' commented Eric.

'It might be, depending on the house they were taken out of,' said Celia.

'If it is a listed property then there are definitely laws against removing architectural features. Unauthorised changes can lead to prosecution, a criminal record, potentially prison and unlimited fines. There is every reason that the Russian would want to keep what he was doing secret,' Ronald said.

Celia looked at Ronald, impressed with his knowledge.

'Well that's what I was not 'appy about,' Monty said.

'Stonepark!' Celia exclaimed.

'That's right luv, well as I said, goes against the grain don't it, I love old houses, take a pride in me work and I know the law. In fact, that was one of the reasons I took this job because I got meself mixed up in something that turned out to be dodgy and when I found out, the people weren't happy about me walking away. Max's offer of a straight up job in Devon came at the right time for me to get out of London for a bit. Turns out that's the best decision I've ever made in me life,' Monty looked down at Lilac as he said these last words.

'Granny's house! Of course, it all makes sense now, the talk of fireplaces and statues - but that would be wicked! Stonepark is a beautiful old manor house! It's part of the history of Devon, it belongs to us, they shouldn't be stripping it to put in some ghastly pleb's house in Surrey!'

'A Pleb? I thought 'ee was a Rusky,' said Fred to Willie.

'I think thicky pleb be a biscuit,' replied Willie, nodding his head with superior knowledge.

Just then Dusty returned with more BIn Gin she had fetched from the bakery.

'Good girl Dusty, let's all raise our glasses to Cat and Tommy. We are coming to rescue you!' Celia held her glass out for more Bin Gin as Dusty was pouring into eager glasses. They all clinked glasses and said in unison,

'Cheers m'dears!'

The Plan

❦

'OK, Dusty, you go and telephone Inspector Pratt. Get him to get some men to Stonepark a.s.a.p. But they had better come in from the widest lane, that's the only one that will accommodate the lorry,' Celia instructed.

'It's OK Dusty, I'll telephone the Inspector. I'll get him to pick me up and I'll show him the way,' said Harold.

'Now, we need to cover all the roads leading away from Stonepark so we can stop the lorry with the goods, just in case Harold and the Inspector don't get there in time.'

Celia was well away, using some of the terms she had read in her crime novels. Ronald rolled his eyes, again, knowing he couldn't stop her but at least she's not putting her life in danger this time, he thought.

'Actually, Monty you probably know the route the lorry is likely to take, bearing in mind it's size, so you take Lilac and see if you can block the road without putting yourselves in danger until the police arrive, Ronald, you go home and fetch the torch and Roley and Polly. If you and Eric follow the route that Tommy usually walks, the girls might be able to pick up the scent or hear Daisy and lead you to her. Betty and Dusty, could you get a flask of strong tea, some blankets and torches, and follow us to Stonepark? Cat and Tommy are going to need some comfort when we find them.'

'Do you really think we will find them Celia?' asked Sharon.

'I'm positive. Now come on, where's that horse of yours?' Celia pushed The Hon Sharon in front of her and followed the others out of the Parish Hall doors. The others all went off to follow Celia's instructions except for Fred and Willie,

'What about me an Willie?' asked Fred.

'You and Willie have the most important job, you can open up the pub as an incident room. Then we can bring everybody back there to recover, and for de-briefing.'

'Cor sounds bootiful, everyone tecking their knickers off in the ole Muff,' Willie chuckled with excitement and anticipation.

Celia Gets a Hand Up

S haron brought her horse, who was jumping about even though she held on tightly to the reins, over to Celia.

'Can you two help Celia up?' Sharon asked Fred and Willie.

'Goodness, lively chap, isn't he? Will he take the weight of both of us?' Celia asked.

'Ere Fred, with a gurt great arse like t'at 'er dun't need a saddle,' Willie said and the two men fell about each other laughing.

The Hon Sharon had already hoisted herself into the saddle and she moved the horse over to the wall of the Parish Hall and next to a bench and called to Celia.

'Come on Celia, climb up on the bench and then if you two chaps could stop laughing for a minute and assist her onto the horse, I would be most grateful,' Sharon politely asked.

Fred and Willie didn't need asking twice. They hauled, pushed and assaulted Celia onto the horse,

'Gwain me bird,' shouted Willie, then they both fell about laughing again.

'I'll deal with you two later,' Celia told them, giving them one of her famous withering looks, which failed to quell the laughter. In fact, it had the opposite effect, but that might have been due to the remains of the Bin Gin, the jar of which Willie had managed to snaffle before Betty left.

Celia Rides Forth

✤✤✤

Celia clung onto the back of The Hon Sharon as they galloped through the darkened village and turned into an even darker lane.

'Can this bloody horse see where it's going in the dark?' screeched Celia in Sharon's ear.

'Yes!' responded Sharon.

'Does he have to go so fishing fast?' Celia yelled, as she flew up into the air and landed back with a simultaneous fanny-fart and thump on her bottom. I don't think this is what they mean by rising to the trot, she thought to herself.

'He doesn't, but I do. I want to save Cat,' Sharon replied over her shoulder whilst kicking her heels, to make the horse go faster.

'Oh f..k it!' Celia thought she might have tiddled herself a bit as she skidded about on the back of the horse. She couldn't see where they were going, which was probably a blessing in disguise due to the speed, as Sharon's hair was blowing out behind her like a curtain in front of Celia's face. Her hands had slipped from Sharon's waist on one of her elevations and now she was clinging to the back of the girl's flimsy silk shirt, hoping that as they made parachutes out of the stuff, it might be strong enough to stop her flying off. What the f..k am I doing on the back of this thing? I must be mad. I'm going to listen to Ronald next time and not get involved!

Just then, a short way in front of them, a helicopter rose up into the air and turned towards the West and the sea.

Sharon slowed a little and Celia managed to speak in her ear, 'Quietly now, we don't want to announce our arrival.'

They slowed down and Sharon steered the horse to the middle of the narrow lane where grass grew down the middle and it could walk quietly. As they drew nearer, they could see a faint light which grew brighter as two full beams from the headlights of a lorry arrived at the top of the drive in front of them. They were dangerously close. Sharon stopped the horse under the shadow of the trees and hoped they wouldn't be seen, but they could see the silhouettes of two men inside the cab of the lorry. There was a panicky moment when the man driving turned his face towards them and, waving a fist and mouthing what was probably best not to know, the lorry turned the other way and rattled off down the lane.

'Let's get down to the house and find Cat and Tommy, I don't think we have anything to worry about now, I think they've left. We can only hope Monty and the police can stop them going any further,' Celia said and they trotted down the drive towards the darkened house.

Sharon pulled the horse on the grass at the bottom of the drive and suggested to Celia, 'I think if you slide off carefully onto the grass Celia, that's the best way down.'

Celia wasn't even sure if she could move! Every muscle in her body was singing and her hands, still tightly clutching handfuls of silk, seemed to have a will of their own and she couldn't open them.

'Might be best to try and get your left leg over at the same time as swinging down onto your tummy, then you can just slide off and it will be a soft landing onto the grass.'

Realising that nothing was happening, and Celia was frozen to the spot, Sharon used her mother's authoritative voice, 'Move Celia!'

Celia did move but unfortunately, she didn't follow instructions and just slid off of the horse sideways. Her right leg landed first, leaving her left leg following behind. Doing the splits as she went down, she still had hold of two handfuls of The Hon Sharon's shirt in a tight grip. Sharon hung on tightly to the reins as she felt herself being pulled backwards and there was the sound of ripping as the material was torn asunder.

'Quickly, there's no time to lose,' Celia said, hoping to distract and gloss over the shirt incident.

Sharon slid of her horse gracefully and tied him to a convenient bush then joined Celia, the shredded remains of her shirt blowing in the breeze as she walked.

Celia Hears a Voice

❦

They tried the front door but as expected it was locked.

'Let's try around the back,' suggested Celia.

'If it's locked I can still get in, through the utility window,' Sharon replied.

The back door was locked and they couldn't see any light or hear any noise from inside the house.

'Are you sure you can get in?' asked Celia.

'Yes, of course. Sometimes when I stayed at my gran's I would sneak out to the stables and sleep with the horses but I had to make sure I was back in my bed before she came to wake me in the morning. The house was locked up last thing at night but the fastener in the utility window is broken and I used to get back in that way.'

With that, Sharon hoisted herself up onto the window ledge, wiggled the window a bit and when it swung open, climbed in. Sharon opened the door, torch in hand, and together they walked in, shining their torches as they went. Celia immediately felt a warmth flooding her body. That's not a hot flush, she thought, I finished with those years ago. She swayed as wisps of images flowed through her consciousness, causing her to feel slightly off balance.

'Do you think it's OK to put the lights on?' whispered Sharon.

It took a moment for Celia to steady herself, she was shaking and felt weird.

'Celia?'

She tried to ground herself, standing still and taking deep breaths. Then she heard the voice.

'Celia? Are you OK?' Sharon reached out in the dark and grabbed a hold of Celia's arm, galvanising her into speech.

'Yes, I'm fine, the electricity might be off but even if it is, we are in no danger now. They have all left,' Celia moved to the light switch and turned the kitchen light on.

'Oh, that's terrible!' Sharon rushed to the fireplace and put her hand on the stone.

'It's not that bad, is it? I take it that's one they have replaced?' Celia asked.

'This was my favourite, it was huge and gran used to let me sit on it and have my breakfast.'

'I am sorry Sharon, but perhaps if Monty and the police can stop the lorry everything can be restored to its rightful place. Even if the Russian owns the house,

I'm guessing that the courts would make him pay for them to be reinstated,' Celia said.

'Anyway, that's not the most important thing, where is Cat and Tommy? Let's have a look at the rest of the house,' Sharon said.

'Well they are here in this house, I am absolutely certain of it, and very near. But you know this house and I don't dear, so where could they have hidden Cat and Tommy?' Celia asked.

'That's supposing they aren't tied up in the back of the lorry,' Sharon said.

'Trust me, they are in this house.'

'How can you be so sure Celia?'

Celia hesitated, but decided she would say it anyway, 'the angel told me.'

'Well, that is good enough for me. I am ready to believe anything if we find Cat safe and well,' and to Celia's surprise, The Hon Sharon hugged her.

'Let's do the ground floor first. We know they are not in here, so let's try the dining room.'

Sharon led the way out of the kitchen but something made Celia hold back. She stood for a while longer before following Sharon around the house.

It took quite a while, but at least there wasn't any furniture left in the rooms which just left the cupboards and storerooms to be searched. After a thorough search the disappointed women went back to the kitchen to wait for either the police or their friends to turn up. Sharon sat on the floor and Celia stood next to the fireplace, leaning on the mantle. Celia's fingers resting on the mantle shelf tingled and she moved away and leant on the wall.

'They *must* be in the lorry with all the stuff. Celia what do we do if the police don't stop them and bring back the Russians and the lorry?

Celia was completely calm, all her anxiety about Cat and Tommy had gone.

'Where could she be Celia? I'm beginning to think the worse, poor Cat,' tears ran down Sharon's face.

Celia moved towards her, leaned down and patted her on the back, then walked to the back door, 'Come on now, I am positive that everything is going to be fine. Why would the Russian take the risk of killing someone just for a few fireplaces and statues? Especially when there will be a paper trail of who bought this place. Plus, there's Monty and Max, they are witnesses to what went on. No, there won't have been any violence. I would think that the Russian buys peoples silence and gets things done by paying for them. Oh, I can hear someone coming, and I think I can hear the motor of a lorry too...'

A Search in the Dark

❧

A car came down the drive, turned at the side of the house and pulled up beside them. Harold stepped out of the driver's seat as a lorry followed him down and drew to a halt behind him. Inspector Pratt, who had been at the wheel, climbed out and stood next to Harold.

'We got them Celia, them pesky Russians, and we've got the loot back. It was so exciting! Donald organised everything, they didn't stand a chance,' Harold beamed, still excited from the chase.

Inspector Pratt, appearing slightly uncomfortable and apprehensive, looked at Celia, but wasn't sure if she was smiling at Harold's enthusiasm or use of his first name.

'We meet again Celia, and according to Harold, we have you to thank for capturing these criminals and stopping them from stealing important artifacts,' he walked forward and held out his hand.

'Well, I don't know about that Inspector, it looks to me as if you are the one who has apprehended them and brought the loot back, but I'm guessing as they aren't with you, that Cat and Tommy weren't in the lorry?' Celia said.

'I am so worried about Cat and Tommy, did Harold tell you they were missing?' asked Sharon.

'And Daisy, yes, I did tell him, but aren't they in the house Celia? I thought that they would be here, locked in a cupboard or something,' Harold looked worried and so now did the Inspector.

'They are here somewhere Harold but Sharon and I have searched the house top to bottom and there is no sign of them,' replied Celia.

'How do you know they are here Celia?' asked Inspector Pratt, but before Celia could answer, Sharon jumped in.

'Actually, Celia, now you've said top to bottom of the house, I've just remembered we didn't search the cellars.'

'Cellars mean old dangerous stairs and spiders to me and I don't do both, so I'll leave that search to you lot,' Celia said firmly.

'And I'll keep Celia company,' Harold said.

'I don't mind spiders and I just want to find Cat, I'll come,' Sharon said.

'I'll do that ladies. I think you have done enough for one night. If you could just point me in the right direction,' the Inspector asked Sharon.

Sharon took him to a door set in in the wall of the

kitchen and the Inspector slid the bolt back before turning to her to ask, 'Have you got a torch?'

'No, but there is light down there, I'll find the light switch,' Sharon found the switch just inside the door and flicked but nothing happened, 'the bulb must have gone,' she said.

'Or somebody's taken it out or broken it, has anybody got a lighter or matches?' asked the Inspector.

They all shook their heads.

'Are there any candles anywhere?' the Inspector persisted.

Celia went to the cupboards under the sink, Harold to a store cupboard and Sharon went to look in the utility room and came back with a very dusty paraffin lamp.

'I remembered Pop's keeping this in a cupboard for emergencies, he sometimes needed it for the stables, it must have been missed in the clear out.'

'Lucky for you Inspector, I didn't fancy your chances in the dark,' Celia said.

Sharon lit the lamp with a match from the box that was with it and they watched as the Inspector and the flickering light disappeared into the darkness down the stairs.

'Why didn't you tell me there was a cellar Sharon? I feel a right idiot, that's more than likely where Cat and Tommy are,' Celia was miffed.

Celia, Sharon and Harold stood around the opened door to the cellar, but couldn't hear a thing.

'Anybody down there Donald?' called Harold but no sound came back.

'Do you think he's alright?' asked Harold.

'Of course he is, he's a trained policeman,' Celia said, but she was a bit worried herself, though not enough to go with him. She'd noticed he had put on a bit of weight since she'd last seen him, probably all those cakes he's been baking she thought.

Then they saw a light and heard his footsteps climbing back up the stairs.

'Nothing down there, and I don't think anybody has been down there for quite a while,' the Inspector said.

'I've got it!' shouted Sharon, 'they must be in the helicopter!'

'Helicopter? What helicopter?' asked the Inspector.

'It was the one that landed by mistake, in the playing field next to the Parish Hall. It had three Russians in it and one was clearly the boss. Then when Celia and I arrived here it had just taken off and it was headed towards Bideford,' Sharon explained.

'Don't worry, I'll get onto the station at Bideford and we'll soon find them,' the Inspector left for his car and police radio, the others waited anxiously inside except for Celia who was strangely calm.

Roley To the Rescue

❦

Betty and Dusty turned up whilst the Inspector was busy on his radio, with flasks of tea and coffee, tins of cake and blankets. Nobody felt like eating but Celia and Sharon were glad of the hot drinks.

'What happened to Monty and Lilac, Harold?' Celia asked.

'What happened to your darling silk shirt sweetie?' Harold asked Sharon, fingering the shreds.

'Forget about clothes for the minute Harold, and tell us what happened!' Celia snapped.

'Yes, sorry Celia. I'm afraid Monty was arrested along with the Russians, and Lilac of course wouldn't leave his side and insisted in going to the police station with him. I did tell Donald that Monty had fessed up and if it hadn't been for him the Russians would have got away with it,' replied Harold.

'Well, that's where I disagree with you Harold. I was well on the way to solving this crime, and even if

Monty hadn't of come forward I know I would have solved it in the end. Still, let's hope they treat him leniently as he did help us. We must make sure and remind the Inspector. Now, where on earth has Ronald got too?' Celia asked, 'I'll go up the drive to the lane and see if he's coming.' Celia crunched her way up the drive, passing the Inspector who was busy talking on his radio. Her eyes had adjusted to the night by the time she had reached the top and she looked in the direction that Ronald should be coming and called.

'Cooee! Ronald!' she was answered by the yapping of her two little dogs in the distance, then she saw Ronald's torchlight illuminating the two dogs who were pulling on their leads in an effort to reach her.

'Everything alright Celia? Did you find Cat and Tommy?' Ronald asked as soon as he had given Celia a hug and a kiss.

'No Ronald but...' Celia's voice trailed off as she knew she was about to say something that might cause Ronald to think she was 50 grams short of a jumper. To delay things for a moment she asked where Eric was.

'Ah well, I think he drank a little too much Bin Gin and you know how it affects people who aren't used to it. The most he has when he's playing with Tommy is two halves a lager. I was worried he was going to fall over and hurt himself, so I've propped him up against a field gate,' Ronald replied.

'Oh goodness, do you think he'll be alright?' Celia asked.

'Of course he will, might be a bit slobbery though.

When I turned back to make sure he hadn't followed me, there was a couple of bullocks leaning over the gate licking his head,' Ronald chuckled.

'Cat and Tommy weren't in the lorry that the police managed to stop, and Sharon and the Inspector seem to think the Russian has taken Cat and Tommy in his helicopter. We saw it take off just as we got here,' Celia explained.

'That doesn't sound very likely to me. I'd have thought he would have left them here and made his escape. He wouldn't want the bother of two people to get rid of, still, if you have searched everywhere,' Ronald was suddenly jerked forward as the dogs pulled on their leads, desperate to get down the drive.

Celia was glad of the distraction delaying what she had been about to tell Ronald.

'The girls want to get inside, they can probably smell Dusty's cake. Come on my lovelies,' Celia took Polly's lead and Ronald held onto Hirsute Roley's, but when they reached the back door of the house, Roley started whining and pulling Ronald away from the house and towards the stables.

'Come on Celia, he's on to something, go on boy,' Ronald unclipped Roley's lead and he shot off. They followed as he disappeared into one of the stables and set up a barking which Polly then joined in with.

'Switch your torch on Ronald, let the dog see the rabbit, so to speak,' Celia said.

They cautiously followed the sounds and found Hirsute Roley, the hero of the hour, dragging an old piece of sacking off away from a pathetic little bundle, lying on the dusty concrete in the corner of one of the stable. Poor Daisy had gaffer tape around her front and back legs and around her muzzle, her eyes were closed and the pink tip of her tongue was just showing out of the tiny gap in her mouth.

'Oh, Ronald, I can't bear it, is she dead?' Celia, with tears in her eyes, tried to pull the two dogs out of the way but there was no way Hirsute Roley was going to move.

'Here, take the torch and we'll get her into the house. I can't risk trying to pull this stuff off out here, it will have to be cut off anyway,' Ronald passed the torch to Celia and gently scooped up the little dog, cradling her to his chest.

Daisy

❦

When they reached the kitchen, everyone was upset to see the state of poor little Daisy. Betty and Dusty rushed to lay some blankets out, Harold filled up one of the flask cups with water from the tap and Ronald laid her down on the blankets.

'Has anyone got a knife or a pair of scissors? I need to get this stuff off and then we can see what's going on,' Ronald asked.

'I brought a cake knife Ronald, will that do?' asked Dusty.

'Is it sharp?'

'Yes, hang on,' she quickly wiped the knife clean of cake and passed it to Ronald.

'Careful Ronald, are you sure you can do it with that safely?' asked Celia.

'It's got to be done. I'll be careful, but we can't leave the poor thing like this. Better she loses a bit of hair than her life.'

'Sorry, you're right, here, I'll hold her,' Celia knelt on the blanket next to Daisy and carefully lifted up her front legs. She tried to pull them apart enough to slide the knife between them but there was no give.

'It's OK, I'm going to slip the tip under just enough to cut the edge, and then I can try and rip it. It's a pity she's not hairy like Roley, there would have been more room, this stuff is stuck tight to her short-coa.' Ronald carefully slid the sharp tip of the knife through the fur on Daisy's leg and managed to make a tiny cut, but try as he might he couldn't get hold of the edges, 'Bugger, my fingers are too big, I can't get a grip, and I don't want to try and cut it anymore,' Ronald sat back on his heels, frustrated that he couldn't release the dog.

'Here, let me, my fingers are smaller but I'm strong,' Sharon said, as she knelt on the rug and took the two tiny exposed edges of the gaffer tape and pulled.

'We only need to split enough to release her legs, we won't take it completely off, better if the vet does that,' Ronald said.

Sharon took the tiny edges stuck with fur and pulled and the tape split, releasing the dogs front legs.

'OK, now for the back legs,' Ronald teased the tip of the knife under the gaffer tape exactly as he did for the front legs and Sharon pulled, splitting it apart.

Daisy still didn't move or respond.

Betty tried to stifle a sob and Harold put one arm around her and the other around Dusty's shoulders.

'C'mon now, Daisy will be alright, Jack Russells' are tough little dogs, with a strong spirit,' Harold said.

'Right, let's get this off her mouth,' it was slightly easier for Ronald to get the knife under this time as there was a bit of a gap, 'Daisy must have been growling when they did this bit because her mouth is slightly open. She doesn't appear to have any other injuries, although she is probably bruised here and there,' Ronald said.

Sharon split the tape around both sides of the little dog's nose and mouth and stroked her face.

'Come on girl, wake up,' Ronald soothed, 'pass me the water Harold,' Ronald asked and with tears in his eyes, he gently trickled some water from his fingers into the side of Daisy's mouth.

Celia and Sharon were massaging her legs, trying to get the circulation back. Suddenly, the little dog's tongue licked at the water Ronald was dripping into her mouth.

'That's it, come on girl, you can do it,' Ronald encouraged her.

'The others joined in murmuring in baby voices, 'who's a boofle girl then, there, there my lovely, open your eyes sweetie.'

The Inspector came back into the kitchen but kept quiet and watched the others trying to coax Daisy back to normality. After a few minutes, the little dog's eyes opened and she struggled to get up, but Ronald lifted her into his lap. Celia struggled to get up and had to accept the strong arms of the Inspector and Harold to help her.

'Any news Inspector?' asked Celia.

'Yes, that's why I was so long, and you were right - your Russian was heading for Bideford where his yacht is moored. According to the Bideford police, he had already caused a lot of local interest. They don't get many luxury yachts moored there, especially ones with helicopter pads on them.'

'So, he's escaped, has he?' Celia asked.

'I'm pleased to say that no, he hasn't. From what I've been told, once the helicopter landed the yacht cast off, and unfortunately for us the tide was with them, otherwise they would have been stuck. But fortunately for us, the MS Oldenburg was returning to Bideford from Lundy, and along with the Appledore and Clovelly lifeboats, they managed to stop them and the lifeboats towed them back into Bideford. The Russians are now in custody, but there was no sign of your two friends on board.'

'I keep trying to tell you, they are here somewhere in the house,' Celia protested.

'I'm happy to search the house, not that I'm doubting you two have made a thorough search, but it wouldn't hurt to look again,' the Inspector agreed, 'let's split up in pairs and perhaps we should check the outbuildings and stables.'

'No, there is no point in looking outside, they are definitely in the house,' Celia was adamant and a little tearful.

The Inspector was curious, 'Why are you so definite they are in the house, Celia?' the Inspector asked.

'Because of the angel.'

She waited for everyone to laugh at her but surprisingly, no one did. They all looked at her expectantly.

'I won't go into it all now, but an angel told me they are here in the house and I'm not leaving until we find them.'

Celia had been pacing the room as she talked but when she stopped found herself at the large fireplace, with Daisy next to her. Whilst everyone had been looking at Celia, they hadn't noticed Daisy climb off Ronald's lap and trot over to join her. Celia's fingers were tingling as they rested on the mantelpiece, and into the silence the voice came again.

'Help Celia, Help.'

Daisy started whining and scrabbling at the fireplace next to Celia.

'They're behind here, Ronald. Behind this fireplace.' Celia said, turning back to the room.

'Don't be absurd, that's a solid fireplace,' said the Inspector.

'I'm telling you, they are behind here,' Celia reiterated calmly.

'Right, let's have a look then,' said Ronald, 'can I borrow the knife again Dusty?'

He took the knife and went to the right of the fireplace, spending some time before leaving it and going around to the left side. After about three minutes there was a click and Ronald called out, 'Harold, come and give me a hand.'

The Inspector joined them, and all three of them

pushed the fireplace out enough for Daisy to dash in behind, yelping with excitement.

Ronald Shone his torch in.

'Ow do buy,' Tommy said from inside the darkened space, 'Give us an 'and with the maid.'

Lost and Found

Harold took the torch and held it whilst Ronald went in and helped Cat out. Betty and Sharon wrapped a blanket around Cat and sat her down on the pile of blankets Daisy had vacated. Sharon sat down next to her and held on tightly whilst murmuring lovingly in her ear, then Betty put a cup of tea in her trembling hand and Dusty cut her a large slice of carrot cake.

Meanwhile, Tommy was being licked to death by Daisy. He was proper angry at the way the little dog had been treated but mighty relieved that the Russians hadn't killed her. Once he could move the dog away from his face, but still holding her tightly in his arms, he spoke to the Inspector,

'There's something you need to see in there, Inspector, I never see it I only felt it but I never told the maid, she don't need to know yet,' Tommy nodded towards Cat.

'Can I have everyone's attention? I think it would be best if everyone made their way home,' the Inspector announced, 'Mrs Bins? Could you and your daughter fit everyone in the back in your delivery van? The dogs too?' he asked.

'Well, I can if you turn a blind eye to me taking dogs in the same place where food is transported,' responded Betty.

'I'll be taking Cat home with me on my horse, she'll be perfectly fine. Cat's van is here somewhere Inspector, do you think it will be safe until we can collect it? Sharon asked.

'I don't think there is any danger of anyone wanting to steal Cat's van. Now go careful, and look after her,' Celia said.

'Celia, you'd better come back with me and Tommy in the Bin's van?' Ronald said.

'No dear, my days of bouncing around in the back of a baker's van like a large bloomer are behind me. I expect the Inspector will bring me back shortly in his car.'

'I don't think I want you to stay here any longer and get mixed up in things, come back with me and the furbabies,' Ronald pleaded, 'we can talk about that new wool you wanted to knit some cushion covers in, what was it now?'

'Nice try Ronald, but I'm staying. We won't be long, and I have the Inspector and Harold with me, go on now,' she gave him a hug and a quick kiss on the cheek. He was only worried about her, she knew.

The Inspector waited till everyone had gone and moved towards the fireplace with Ronald's torch in hand. Celia moved with him and said,

'I'll come in with you Inspector, another pair of eyes and all that.'

'Are you sure? Because I'm not sure what we are going to find?' the Inspector replied.

'I was a Girl Guide Inspector, always prepared, I'll be fine. Let's get it over with.'

'What do you think this place was for Celia?' the Inspector asked as he switched the torch on and prepared to go in.

'Probably a priest's hole. This is an old Devon Manor house. At the time of religious persecution some families still held secret religious services and the consequences of being discovered were horrendous so they devised these hiding places to protect themselves and their priests.'

The Inspector, embarrassingly, couldn't quite squeeze through the gap and the three of them had to make it wider, which suited Celia as she had wondered if she could manage to get in the small gap herself. Celia followed the Inspector, and once she had stepped in she immediately felt an atmosphere and the air turned a couple of degrees colder. Looking around the Inspector's bulk, Celia followed the light of the torch, but for a moment couldn't quite take in what she was seeing.

'Celia, can you turn around and make your way out? I'm right behind you,' the Inspector said.

The Inspector and Celia looked at each other as they stepped back into the kitchen.

'What is it? What did you find?' asked Harold.

'Skeletal remains, possibly human,' answered the Inspector.

'I think, quite definitely human, from what I saw, 'Celia added.

'So not anything to do with the Russians then?' asked Harold.

'I can't rule it out at this stage, but I think we will find that they have been there a very long time. I'm going out to call it in, but I don't believe anything will happen tonight, this is an old crime. It is a crime scene of course, God knows what forensics are going to make of it. The whole world and his dog have been in this house tonight,' the Inspector walked out of the kitchen and Harold followed him.

Celia Finds an Angel

❧❀❧

'Many a thing twixt heaven and earth'

Shakespeare
         Celia was drawn back to the priest hole. She stepped behind the fireplace, into the darkness. The only illumination was the light from the kitchen. She drew her cardigan closer against the chill. There was no sound. It was very still, as if even the air failed to move. She didn't really want to go in too far, the thought of the fireplace closing and plunging her into darkness was terrifying. Darkness wasn't Celia's favourite thing.

'OK, you are fine, there's light from the kitchen. Breathe, in out, in out...' Celia told herself, trying to suppress the slight panic she could feel rising through her body, 'in out, in out.' The combination of the dark place and the possibility of spiders was about to be too much for Celia. But, as suddenly as she had been plunged into darkness and fear, it lifted. She felt calm, her breathing slowed and her shoulders dropped from her ears.

A light! There was a faint aquamarine glow about halfway along the wall and two thirds of the way down. Celia moved slowly towards the light, one hand sliding along the wall, all thoughts of spiders forgotten as she was drawn towards the glow.

Shockingly illuminated were two small clothed female skeletons. She knew they were female from the hair on their sunken skulls and their clothes. One had plaits resting on her shoulders. You could still see their skin and fingernails. She only had a little knowledge about this kind of thing, but she assumed that as they were sealed in what was virtually a tomb, the bodies hadn't putrefied as they would if they were exposed to the air.

They were lying on their sides facing each other, arms entwined, with something lying between them. Celia moved as close as she could without touching them and saw the most heartbreaking sight of all, the body of a tiny baby wrapped in a bit of old flannel.

A feeling of sorrow swelled through her body and filled the chamber. Tears poured from her eyes, but she couldn't move. It was one of the saddest things she had ever seen. What tragedy occurred that these three had ended their days in this cold airless tomb?

The light seemed to glow brighter as she looked across and saw a small niche in the plaster, the light was coming from inside. She stood and moved around the bodies until she was close to the niche. Inside was a tiny painted naive figure, dressed in blue with some sort of silver bonnet. Celia reached in and lifted the small figure out, cupping it gently in her hand. It was made of some sort of clay and had a plain, but most serene face. On its back were a perfect set of wings.

'Blessings from the Angel of Presence.'

Celia heard those words as clearly as if someone had spoken them out loud. She nearly dropped the figure as she stood up, shocked, and moved towards the entrance. Almost stepping out into the kitchen, something stopped her. She looked down at the tiny angel in her hand and felt a wellspring of understanding. Swiftly, moving back into the priest's hole, she bent and placed the tiny figure back in its small niche. Back at the opening, she turned and looked back. There was no light. In fact, she couldn't even see a niche anymore. Nobody would believe what had happened, she thought, unless they'd heard, or seen it with their own ears and eyes. I suppose that will be the last of my angel dreams.

The Inspector came back into the Kitchen, 'are you coming Celia? Harold's already in the car, I'll lock up and forensics will be all over this in the morning,' he said.

'What happened to Max Cheetham?' asked Celia.

'Who's he?' asked the Inspector.

'Nobody important, I don't want to think about it all anymore, I just want to go home.'

Bin Gin recipe

COURTESY OF BETTY BIN

Sterilized jar with sealed lid

One bottle of Gin - must be Juniper Gin or Sloe Gin at Christmas

1 box of Golden Raisins

Put raisins in the jar, pour in the gin, cover and leave for 1 -2 weeks or until raisins have drunk the gin and plumped up.

EAT EXACTLY 9 A DAY FOR MEDICINAL PURPOSES
     Or DRINK A SMALL TOT IN AN EMERGENCY

This recipe belongs to the Bin family, they are happy to share it with you but refuse permission to make it commercially.

Just in Case You Are Interested...

St Urith was a Brythonic maiden. The Britons were an ancient Celtic people who lived in Britain from the Iron Age through the Roman and Sub-Roman periods. They spoke a language that is known as Common Brittonic. Legend says that Saint Urith was born at East Stowford in Swimbridge Parish in North Devon, England. She was converted to Christianity and lived as a hermit in Chittlehampton, North Devon where she founded a church.

There are stories that say she was cut down either by: A rampaging haymaking gang of scythe wielding village maidens who were bribed to kill her by her wicked pagan stepmother, or by a fleet of marauding Vikings. I think it is fair to say either could be true and we'll never know for certain. It is said that a fountain sprung up from the ground where her head fell and there is still a well there in the village to this day.

According to the Appledore History Society there

are ancient records of Northam written in the 10th/11th century containing a traditional story that says:

'Hubba the Dane' arrived with a fleet of 33 ships and marched to attack the Hill Fort at Kenwith. Legend states that they were defeated by Odun, Earl of Devon, he and 1000 of his men were killed. The men were buried at Bonehill and Odun in a cairn known as Hubbastone.

Today, if you drive from Northam to Appledore in North Devon you will come across a Stone tablet at Bloody Corner, erected by Charles Chappell, which says:

Stop Stranger Stop,
Near this spot lies buried
King Hubba the Dane,
Who was slayed in a bloody retreat,
By King Alfred the Great.

There is also an area in 'The Copse', Northam Woods, which is called King Alfred's Cave and is reputed to be where King Alfred hid when being chased by the Vikings.

So, it is possible Saint Urith was killed by an early Viking raid. Her feast day is the 8th July and Saint Urith's holy well still stands at the east end of Chittlehampton, North Devon, England.

With thanks to The Appledore History Society and to Trinity College Library, Cambridge.

Devon Dialect

There are very many different ways of saying the same thing depending on which part of Devon you live in and sometimes from village to village. Not everyone in St Urith speaks in the wonderful 'Nor Debbn' dialect and it would be hard work to read too much of it. There are some characters, however, that will not allow me to write it any other way: 'Willie' being one.

Nor' Debben - North Devon

Thicky - that.

Dreckly - directly.

Ort - anything.

Buy - boy.

Maid - girl

If you would like to know more about the Devon dialect an excellent book is:

'Cheers Me Boodies' by John Germon

Thanks

My thanks to Gill and Vicky Morrish who gave me invaluable advice about the Hon Sharon's horse.

Many thanks to my friend Terri Everitt for reading the book and giving me honest feedback.

Huge thanks to my son Adam Barnett for all the technical wizardry stuff and getting the book published I couldn't do it without him.

Tremendous thanks to my daughter Sally Barnett for her insightful and invaluable suggestions and for her brilliant editing.

Special thanks to my husband Roger who feeds and looks after me when I can't stop writing.

I am so lucky to have such loving support from my family, Cherry Barnett, Sonya Barnett, Livyy, Iceni, Myo and Sally and Adam mentioned above.

17269736R00141

Printed in Great Britain
by Amazon